"Deliciously romantic! After reading *Falling for a Real Cowboy*, I wanted to book a casita on Vargas Ranch for a month. The Arizona setting came to life, and I had all the feels while watching River and Dalton fall in love. A terrific start to a memorable series."

–Jill Kemerer, *Publishers Weekly Bestselling Author*

Falling for a Real Cowboy

Vargas Ranch Book 1

Karen Baney

desert life
media

Falling for a Real Cowboy: Vargas Ranch Book 1
By Karen Baney

Publisher:
Desert Life Media, LLC
Gilbert, AZ 85295

www.karenbaney.com

Printed in the United States of America

ISBN 978-1-960217-07-3

With regard to the works of man,
by the word of your lips
I have avoided the ways of the violent.
My steps have held fast to your paths;
my feet have not slipped.

Psalms 17:4-5

1

"Look, River, I'm not suggesting we would fire you. You're still one of our most popular authors."

River Sloane's shoulders dropped, and her heart squeezed tight as she waited for the "but" she knew was coming. She heard it in her publisher's tone on the phone call. The muscles in her neck tightened. She wished she had let the call go to voicemail.

"But *Frenemy Journalists* is performing far below expectations. *Dueling Doctors* is doing better than it, but still not great. We need another big hit from you."

Or else. She could hear the insinuation. River's face heated as her anxiety rose. She desperately needed to write another bestseller, and fast. She held back a sigh as Kendra Browning, her publisher, pressed forward.

"Cowboy romances are *the* rage."

River drummed her fingers against the smooth wood finish on her writing desk, staring out the one lone window as the skies darkened. For half a second, she debated how to respond.

"No. I don't do country, cowboys, or small towns. That doesn't fit with my brand," she argued. "City life is what my readers expect."

"Cowboy, country, and small towns are all part of our brand. Anything remotely related to cowboys flies off the shelves. It's that or Amish romance."

River held up a finger to her mouth and pantomimed gagging. Thankfully, it wasn't a video call. Amish was by far the worst option in her mind. At least she had read some of the cowboy romance coming out of her publisher and kinda liked them.

"So, which will it be? Cowboy or Amish?"

"What about vacation romance?" she suggested as her throat constricted and her cheeks flushed. She couldn't lose her contract. It would take too long to establish herself with a new publisher. Although she could become an independent author. She had an enormous fan base. Except for one major problem—she still owed her publisher three more novels.

"If it's a vacation romance on a guest ranch with cowboys, then I'm all for it."

River frowned as the bile crawled up her throat. None of it sounded good to her. She knew nothing about cowboys or ranches. At least she had spent a few summers on her grandparents' farm and knew a little about animals.

"In fact, Angela has already booked you a six-week stay at a guest ranch…"

Kendra's voice was muffled as she asked the name of the place.

"Vargas Guest Ranch & Resort in Wickenburg, Arizona. Angela has you flying out from Columbus tomorrow at seven."

"What?" River bit her lip. Surely, Kendra joked.

"We've already arranged for you to learn from the cowboys what ranch life is really like. Since it's off-peak season for them, they agreed to show you the ropes." Kendra snorted before she giggled. "Ha. Ropes."

River did not find Kendra's accidental pun amusing at all. A ranch in the middle of nowhere in Arizona. In June. If it was hot in Ohio, how hot would it be in Arizona? Maybe she ought to reconsider the Amish subgenre. Then she could stay in Ohio and drive to a working Amish farm.

"Go. Have fun. Get a massage. Then put on some cowboy boots and jeans and learn all you can. When you've got something to share, our editors will be ready to read it. I'm hoping you'll get something to me by the end of July."

Six weeks. River swallowed a sip of her iced tea as Kendra disconnected the call. Six weeks didn't seem long enough to become inspired to write something she had almost no interest in.

As she padded to her bedroom, she shook her head and muttered, "Cowboy romance."

Digging her luggage out of the closet, she stared at her wardrobe. What did they consider ranch attire? Not her leggings or sweat pants. Probably not her dress slacks and silky tops she wore to book signings.

With a few taps on her phone, River pulled up the ten-day forecast for Wickenburg. Hot, hotter, and sizzling. Was she going to the surface of the sun? She had never been to a place warmer than ninety degrees. She finger combed her long blond hair before flipping it over her shoulder. Grabbing four sundresses, she dropped them in her large suitcase. Then she gathered every pair of shorts she owned. A half hour later, she had two pairs of sandals, tennis shoes, and tons of clothes stuffed into the enormous suitcase. She really hated checking her bags, but no way around it with a six-week trip.

An email notification chimed on her phone from Kendra's assistant with her travel itinerary. River scanned the departure times as she flopped onto her recliner. Six weeks. In some place called Wickenburg, clear across the country from Columbus, Ohio. She groaned.

If she wanted to keep her job, she had better find the motivation to make this assignment work. Except writing was as much art as mechanics. When she wasn't inspired and ideas weren't flowing, staring at her laptop screen, even on location, would not produce a story from her dejected heart.

Lord, help me find my muse again. I love writing. I love tell-ing stories about couples falling in love who grow deeper with You. But cowboys? I just don't think I can do it.

When River's phone played the Doctor Who theme song, she rubbed circles on her temples. Then she answered it on the third ring.

"Hey Mom."

"I sensed something is wrong and thought I should call."

River was used to her mom's uncanny ability to know when she needed to talk. Though River attributed it to God intervening, her mom would probably claim it was because she had read some crystals. River knew better. She knew God loved her and even if her parents weren't Christians, she still listened to her mother's wisdom and tuned out the weird.

Expelling a loud breath, River told her mom all about her dilemma.

"Ooo. I wish I could go. I'd love to spend a month on a dude ranch. Ray! River is going to Arizona to a *dude* ranch!"

River punched the speaker button while she ordered Chinese takeout from an app. Who knew when she would get authentic lo mein again? Seriously, she could live off chicken or beef lo mein. It was practically a food group.

"Your father is jealous, too. Anyway, honey, I think the idea of a cowboy romance is wonderful. Write something steamy and you'll have a big hit. Maybe your biggest hit yet. And your name—River Sloane—it even sounds western!"

Not this again. River refused to compromise her integrity by writing the smutty stuff her mom read, even though she wasn't thrilled about writing a cowboy romance. River liked clean romance. Lots of kissing, but no heat. It fit with her style and that of her publisher. And she could include Chris-tian themes, which had always felt like a calling from God.

Her doorbell rang, giving her a reason to end the con-versation. She gave her parents her love. They promised to check on her place while she was gone.

After retrieving the bag of food from her porch, she breathed deeply of the garlic and ginger aroma. Her stomach growled as she slid onto a stool at the kitchen bar. While she downed her noodles, she propped her phone on a holder on the black quartz countertop and clicked the link to the Vargas Guest Ranch & Resort. A picture of five gorgeous cowboys in their twenties and thirties conveyed the authentic western vibe of the place. She studied their faces and compared them to the older couple on the right. Family. The serious-looking brother captured her attention. Gold eyes. Ruggedly handsome face. His crossed muscular arms pulled his plaid shirt taut. Hmm. Maybe visiting the ranch wouldn't be so bad after all.

When River read the "about us" page, sure enough, it was family owned and operated. The pictures of the couples' casitas oozed western with its distressed painted walls and wood log beams on the ceiling. A rustic wood desk stood in front of a window with a lovely view of a craggy mountain. Worst case, she would end up on a relaxing vacation right before they fired her. If she didn't find her muse.

Perhaps she ought to come up with a backup plan. She could always fall back on her marketing degree and graphic design experience. River had maintained a relationship with a few clients over the years and occasionally picked up some freelance work. It might pay the bills.

After she finished her lo mein, she cringed as she tossed the extra in the trash. It would have made a tasty lunch during a busy writing day. She took the trash bag out to the dumpster. Then she packed the last of her things before turning in for the night.

THE MOMENT RIVER stepped out of the airport in Phoenix, Arizona, the heat blasted her face like an oven set to five hundred degrees. Her skin felt like it would char any second and she wasn't even in the sun. Sweat dotted her forehead by the time she walked across the parking garage to the ride share pickup area. Thankfully, Kendra's assistant had reserved the ride share for her.

River greeted the young man who barely looked old enough to have a license, much less meet the twenty-one-year-old age requirement. Maybe he was one of those guys that looked sixteen but was really thirty.

"Headed to Wickenburg?" Max asked.

"Yes, the Vargas Guest Ranch & Resort."

With a grunt, Max hefted her luggage into the trunk of his Corolla, the weight causing a loud thud as it hit the bottom. Thank goodness it was a hardshell case. Then he held open the back door as she scooted in. Once she buckled up, he pulled out. The overpowering fake new car air freshener made her eyes burn.

Glancing at the clock on his dash, she made sure her watch and phone switched to the correct time zone. Eleven in the morning or two her time. No wonder her stomach growled. She should have bought something for lunch at the airport. Oh well.

River watched as they drove through the city on the surface streets. Many stuccoed buildings were painted in varying bland shades of tan. Instead of green grass in the easement, tan gravel and tiny bushes lined the streets. Boring.

Eventually, they left the city behind. Small bushes, dirt, and tall green cacti covered the expansive land on both sides of the two-lane highway. In the distance, brown mountains lent variation to the horizon against a brilliant blue sky.

After more than an hour driving outside of the metro area, Max asked her where the place was again. She told him as they entered the Wickenburg city limits.

"That's another thirty minutes beyond Wickenburg. I can't go that far. I have another fare at one."

"You have to. My company paid for you to take me to the ranch."

"No can do, lady. I'll drop you here at the grocery store. I'm sure someone from the ranch can come pick you up."

As he stopped the car in the parking lot of the store, River's throat constricted. The town of Wickenburg didn't look like much. She doubted she could book another ride share or taxi. When Max held the door open, the hot air rolled over her in a wave, like she had stuck her face under a hand dryer in a gas station bathroom. She crossed her arms over her chest and shook her head. He left the car door wide open and rounded to the trunk to retrieve her luggage.

"Get out," he commanded.

She was pretty sure she could take the young rail of a man.

"Now, lady."

River huffed and exited the vehicle. The tires barked as Max pealed out. She frowned at his brake lights. Just as soon as she found a way to the ranch, she would leave him a nasty review. Ugh. No, she wouldn't. She didn't have a vengeful bone in her body.

Shoppers hurried into the grocery store. As the sun seared her exposed arms, River understood their haste. The heat felt oppressive. She dragged her luggage to a spot in the shade. It wasn't any cooler.

Now, what was she going to do?

DALTON VARGAS RAN a hand through his short, dark hair before jamming the Stetson back on his head. The meeting with the Independent Rustic Lodging Association went well. Or it would have, had it not been for Howard. Most of the Maricopa County chapter liked his idea of a joint website to promote all the members' accommodations. He advised centralizing the reservations, which would improve the online experience for guests. By pooling their resources, they could hire someone to build a nicer website than most of the owners could afford on their own.

Despite their excitement, Howard Pollard didn't like the idea. He owned a small working ranch and a guest ranch on the northern side of Wickenburg. He had countered every one of Dalton's points, winning over a few members. Howard always found some reason to oppose anything Dalton suggested. The man's intense distrust towards him was a mystery, as he did not know what caused it.

He pushed the start button on his shiny new Ford F-350 super duty, immediately followed by the AC. The engine hummed to life with a manly sound that made him want to drive for hours. He snorted. He had an almost two-hour drive ahead of him back to the ranch. Good thing he loved driving his new truck.

Dalton turned on the sound system and played his favorite country playlist. The music improved his mood by the time he made it out of the metro area. The saguaro cacti stood like guards over the scrub brush. Distant mountains rose from the desert and cut sharply into the blue sky. He would never tire of the scenic desert drive.

The next worry on his internal list gnawed at him. Since Vargas Ranch straddled the border of Maricopa and Yavapai Counties, he held membership in both chapters. The Yavapai County chapter might be more reluctant to take part in his joint website idea. They didn't have deep pockets. Dalton planned to cover whatever cost the two chapters couldn't. He had already budgeted for the entire project out of the Vargas Ranch funds. Both the cattle ranch and resort were doing well. They had had an excellent spring season this year after several slim ones.

Papi told him a few weeks ago how proud Dalton's management of the ranch made him. It was good to hear, even if he spent many evenings butting heads with his old man over his plans to improve and expand the ranch. Papi and Padre, Dalton's grandfather, didn't always like his "newfangled" ideas.

Dalton growled. Why had they sent him to Arizona State University for an MBA if they expected him not to use it? Maybe one day they would let him manage the place as he saw fit.

From the time he was old enough to walk, they had groomed Dalton to take over the ranch. At thirty-four, he handled all the operations for the ranch and resort. Things ran well as long as they agreed with his ideas.

However, this morning at breakfast, Papi told him and his four brothers he planned to take the summer off. Then in September, Papi wanted to help Mami in the garden and with beautification of the resort grounds. Dalton snorted. At fifty-six, Papi was effectively retiring early to become the landscaper. His father had always loved planting things.

Just like him, Papi had been groomed to run the place. Papi had taken over when Dalton's grandfather had turned fifty. Grandfather had had a heart attack, thrusting Papi into managing the ranch by himself in his early thirties, while raising five sons.

At least Dalton didn't have to worry about supporting a wife and kids. Janessa, his ex-fiancée, had done a number on him. So much that he decided marriage wasn't for him. He was married to the ranch. If other women were like Janessa, he had missed nothing by staying single.

Of course, Mami reminded him often that she wanted grandchildren. He would have liked to tell her to nag Dylan or Derin. His next two younger brothers had been single for a long time. Surely one of them could fall in love and grant Mami the desire of her heart. Because there was no way Dalton would open his heart again.

His phone rang, and he punched the hands free button on his steering wheel.

"Hey Renata," he greeted his younger cousin, who managed the reservations for the guest ranch.

"Hey, have you gone through Wickenburg yet?"

"Just on the outskirts now."

"Oh, good!" Renata's breath whooshed loudly over his speakers. "Can you stop by Safeway?"

"Um, did Chef run out of something?" It wasn't like him to do so. And odd that he would send Dalton to a regular grocery store instead of the restaurant supply store.

"No. Nothing like that. Remember how I told you about the romance author at breakfast this morning?"

"Yeah?" Sometimes he wished Rennie would get to a point twice as fast as she normally did.

"Well, it seems her ride share driver didn't realize he would lose half his day driving out here. She's stranded at Safeway."

"In this heat?" Hopefully, she had the sense to purchase some water.

"When I called the store manager, he said he'd let her wait in his office until you showed up."

"Alright. Text him I'm about fifteen minutes out."

"Thanks Dalton. You're the best."

He snorted. The whole romance author thing annoyed him. Some city slicker who had never set foot on a ranch was gonna hang out and learn from the cowboys of Vargas Ranch. Silly notion. She probably didn't even own a pair of cowboy boots.

Seemed Mami, Renata, and his other cousin Solana knew the writer. They said she was famous. What would he know about it? Romance wasn't his thing. Not in fiction, and certainly not in life after Janessa shredded his heart. Give him a good business book or colonial American story and he would be happy. Not that he had time to read.

He slowed his truck as he turned into the grocery store parking lot. The moment he spotted her, he swallowed hard. Her blond hair glowed in the sunlight. The bright blue sundress fit her to perfection, showing off her pale ivory skin and shapely legs. Exactly his type. Why did she have to be blond? And stunning.

As Dalton shifted into park, he sipped his water, watching the stranger from the safety of his truck. When she glanced up, his heart rate spiked. Her smile slowly appeared when he opened his truck door.

"Miss Sloane?"

She let out a rush of air before flashing him a gorgeous smile. His heart did funny things. He needed to get a grip.

"Oh, good. You must be Dalton. Renata worried she might miss catching you."

Dalton introduced himself and extended his hand for a shake, noting how soft her skin felt against his rough fingers.

"Just call me River."

Rarely—maybe never—had he called a guest by their first name. It seemed almost unprofessional.

"Can I take your bags?" he asked, motioning to the purple bags.

A nervous laugh escaped her pink lips. Those hazel eyes muddled his brain for a few seconds. Inwardly shaking it off, he leaned down, grabbed the suitcases, and slid them into the back seat. Then he held the passenger door open for her.

"Need some water before we go?"

"The store manager hooked me up. Thanks."

He waited to close the door until she buckled up. Then he rounded the truck and eased behind the wheel. Her sweet fragrance smelled amazing. The sundress she wore showed off her slender arms and the blue color suited her, bringing out the blue flecks in her hazel eyes. Dalton focused on the road ahead of them, willing his pulse to slow.

"Kinda fancy duds for a cowboy," River said.

He had worn a suit jacket with his dress jeans and a blue button-down shirt. The association meetings and church on Sunday were the only times he really looked like a business owner.

"I had a meeting in town."

"Here in Wickenburg?"

"Nope. North Phoenix."

"Oh."

She went silent and stared out the passenger window as her perfume nearly drove him mad. He needed a distraction, so he struck up a conversation.

"Is this your first time in Arizona?"

"Yes."

He snorted. "You came at the hottest time of year. June through most of September is scorching."

"So I'm realizing."

Silence again as she repositioned the vents to blast AC in her face. The force caused her silky blond hair back in gentle waves. He swallowed hard.

Dalton glanced over at her. She fidgeted with her fingernails, then picked at lint on her dress. Nervous, not excited. Odd. Most of their guests couldn't contain their enthusiasm over staying at a working ranch.

"What brings you to our ranch?" he asked, even though he knew she had to complete research for her book.

"Oh, I'm here to save my job. I hope."

The forlorn tone of her voice triggered his instinct to fix things for her.

No. He should not get involved with a woman. Especially a guest, no matter how pretty she looked.

The quiet returned after her odd answer. He nudged the accelerator until his vehicle moved a little above the speed limit, hoping to make it to the dirt road turnoff sooner. Awkward didn't being to describe the mood in his truck.

A soft gasp escaped her mouth when the mountain came into view. His mountain. His home.

"What's it called?" she asked.

Dalton cleared his throat as heat crept up his neck and settled over his face. It suddenly felt weird to say the name aloud.

"Dalton Peak."

2

RIVER LAUGHED UNCONTROLLABLY until tears formed in the corners of her eyes. She swiped her fingers under them to remove the moisture from her cheeks.

"You named a mountain after yourself?"

The act seemed the opposite of the quiet cowboy's demeanor. She slanted toward him as her laughter faded. She studied his ruggedly handsome, tanned face and angular jaw. He looked ten times manlier in person than in the picture. Those gold eyes—the ones she had stared at too long on the website picture—hid behind aviator sunglasses, which seemed out of place with the rest of his western attire. Maybe he was a closet *Top Gun* fan or something.

Red spread up his neck and onto his perfectly handsome cheeks. She found his embarrassment endearing.

"It's named after my great-grandfather, Dalton J. Vargas, Sr."

River arched a brow. So not this Dalton, but another one?

"My grandfather is Dalton J. Vargas, Jr., who we call Padre. My father? He's the third. Goes by Tres."

"Trace?"

"No, tres. For the third. I'm Dalton J. Vargas the fourth."

"Wow. That's got to be confusing."

River covered her smirk with her hand. This cowboy was full of quirks—ones she couldn't wait to jot down and use in a story. Wait, did she just admit she might want to write about a cowboy? Naw. Must be the heat frying her brain.

"Not really. We call grandpa Padre. Papi is just Papi to us boys. Mami calls him Tres. So I'm the only Dalton."

"Huh." She barely followed it all.

The sound of gravel crunching under the tires blended with the hearty rumble of the engine as he pulled onto the dirt drive. The conversation came to an awkward pause.

River's gaze roamed over the short, green-trunk trees as they drove by. Beautiful golden flowers covered their branches. A sandy swath carved a sunken path between the rows of trees. Beyond what looked like banks, though no water flowed anywhere, small bushes dotted the dusty landscape.

"That's Vargas Wash." Dalton's deep voice broke the silence.

Go figure. Something else named after the cowboy. Or his family.

"Wash? As in water?"

"Not at the moment. When the monsoon storms kick in, rushing water fills and often overflows the wash bed. If that happens, don't cross it. Not even in a vehicle."

So serious, this Dalton J. Vargas the fourth. It couldn't be that bad. Right now, it looked completely harmless.

"I've seen vehicles bigger than mine swept away. Folks drown. Horses too."

River laughed nervously. "Point taken, cowboy."

The dirt drive curved to the right. Suddenly, a series of stucco buildings came into view. The turquoise pool glimmered in the early afternoon sun. Tan umbrellas stood tall between poolside lounge chairs. A fine mist emanated from the roofline of the patio. Must be an Arizona thing.

She spotted a sign for the spa. "You have a spa?"

Visions of massages filled her mind's eye. Mmm. She could use a little rest and relaxation. Maybe some pampering, too.

"For the women guests. Seems they love their mani-pedis and massages. Though some of the male guests like the massages too. Renata convinced me to open it last year. Turned out to be so popular that we're hiring a second massage therapist for the fall season."

The entire conversation puzzled River. She never expected a cowboy to take such an interest in the resort part of the property.

"Exactly what do you do here?" she asked.

"I'm the Ranch Manager. Basically, the CEO of the ranch, accommodations, dining hall, events, and resort."

Her jaw dropped. "All that?"

A small smile tugged on one corner of his mouth. "Yeah. It's a multi-million-dollar enterprise."

"No way!"

Dalton cleared his throat as he jammed the shifter into park. "Here we are. I'll keep the AC running if you want to hop out and check in. Then I can drive you over to the casita."

"Drive?" How far away was it?

"It's a bit of a walk from here and I—" he nodded toward her feet. "Don't think flip-flops will be comfortable for that walk in this heat."

River's cheeks warmed. Another concern added to her plate. Hopefully, her tennis shoes would be adequate for her stay.

She quickly opened the door and slid to the ground. The seat of the truck came to her chest. Such a huge, fancy vehicle. Guess CEO of the ranch paid well. Certainly explained the luxurious interior. She closed the truck door and walked toward the red-painted stucco building.

When she opened the glass doors, a young woman, nearly ten years her junior, greeted her with a smile.

"River Sloane! I can hardly believe you're really here. At our ranch. Oh, my gosh. Aunt Catalina is going to freak out when she meets you. She's such a fan."

Being famous brought with it many uncomfortable conversations like that. All she wanted was her room key and a giant bucket of ice. River rubbed the back of her hand on her forehead, then on the side of her dress. She felt like she had already sweat a gallon. Maybe once she cooled down, she might want to eat.

By the time Solana checked her in, the AC finally cooled her skin. Just in time to venture into the sweltering heat again. Ugh.

River darted toward the truck and stopped short when she heard Dalton on the phone.

"Thanks Randy. I'll figure out how to stop it from leaking more." He waved her in. "Please let me know if you can't make it out in the morning."

After River settled in the truck seat, Dalton turned toward her.

"The kitchenette in your casita is leaking. I know we have a water shut off under it. Would you prefer we move you to the other one? If we do, you'll have to move after the second week of your stay. We have a honeymooning couple that asked for the other casita specifically."

"Does the rest of the plumbing work?"

"Yeah, you can use the bathroom. Just not the kitchenette sink."

"Let's go then."

She watched in awe as he effortlessly backed the massive truck out of the parking spot one-handed. The trip to her casita only took a few minutes. They had painted the beautiful stucco building a homey shade of yellow, complementing the rustic dark wood logs on the porch. Smaller logs provided a simple railing. A brightly colored God's eye patterned rug laid in front of the dark wood door. Three small frosted windows topped the upper third of the door. She pressed the key card to the pad on the wall and turned the black wrought iron door knob. The smell of vanilla and cinnamon greeted her as she walked inside, instantly calming her.

"Where would you like your luggage?"

Dalton's deep voice stirred her from her appreciation of the welcoming, southwestern decor. "Bedroom is fine."

Heat warmed her cheeks at the thought of the tall, broad-shouldered cowboy in her bedroom. Okay. The appeal of a cowboy romance novel suddenly made sense. Still, she didn't know if *she* could enjoy writing one.

The cowboy shed his tan hat from his head as he entered the living area. His dark, mussed hair stood every which way, begging her to smooth it. She resisted the urge, clasping her hands in front of her.

"This place is immense," River said as she turned in a circle.

"You should see the family casitas. Those make this look like a closet."

"Maybe I could see one of them sometime — if there are no guests."

"Just ask Renata or Solana. I'm sure they'd love to take you on a tour."

As Dalton swayed from cowboy-booted foot to foot, River gave him her full attention, raising her eyebrows.

"Would you mind if I look at the kitchenette sink while I'm here? The plumber will be here tomorrow, but Renata said it needs attention today."

"Go ahead. I'll just unpack my things and settle in."

He entered the kitchenette as she headed into the bedroom. Unable to relax with the hunky cowboy just a room away, she hefted her suitcases onto the bed and emptied them. She frowned at her choice of clothes. Even the women working in the office wore jeans. She had seen no one in shorts yet, despite the heat.

River figured she might need to buy a few things for her stay. Time would tell. Hopefully, they'd let her relax the rest of today before putting her to work.

DALTON TOOK OFF his tailored suit jacket and carefully laid it on the back seat of his truck. Then he rolled his blue executive shirt sleeves above his elbows. Right then, he wished he had thought to stow a work shirt in his truck this morning. Made little sense to drive all the way over to the family ranch house just to change his shirt and come back to stop the leak.

He opened the built-in tool chest in the truck bed and grabbed his toolbox and a bucket before dropping the metal lid closed with a clank. Then he headed into the casita, pausing for a few seconds when he caught sight of River through the doorway of the bedroom. His mouth felt drier than Vargas Wash.

She sure was gorgeous. Not the least bit pretentious, like he had envisioned this morning. She had a great sense of humor, too. When she glanced up and smiled, he ducked his head and scurried toward the kitchenette, pulse dancing.

Dalton crouched down in front of the sink. The mildew smell stung his nostrils. Water slowly dripped from the cabinet door. As he kneeled in front of it, the water soaked through his jeans. Crud.

He dug a flashlight from his toolbox and shone it at the pipes. Finding the water shut-off valves, he turned them and sent a prayer heavenward that it would stop the leak. He waited a few seconds. No new water drops. Thank goodness.

After stowing his flashlight in the toolbox, he stood and crossed to the locked linen closet in the hallway. The keys jingled softly as he thumbed through them before he finally unlocked it. He grabbed a stack of towels and pressed them down onto the standing water in the cupboard. With a quick flick of his wrist, he tossed the wet towels into the bucket, causing a splattering sound.

He texted Solana. *Send towels over to River's casita. Tell housekeeping to mop the floor.*

Solana texted back: *River's casita?* With a winking emoji.

Heat crawled up his neck because of his mistake. He should have called it the Cholla Casita.

Wiping his hands on one of the slightly damp towels in the bucket, he stood. Then he hovered in the bedroom's doorway. Strange jitters danced in his chest. *Get a grip.* It was just an attraction. He should ignore it.

"All fixed for now. What's your number?"

River tossed her head back and laughed, a deep, throaty sound. Heat spread across his face again.

"Do you ask all your single female guests for their numbers?"

About that sense of humor... "So I can let you know when the plumber arrives tomorrow. We'll need access for an hour, and I don't want to surprise you."

Those hazel eyes sparked with mirth. "I like surprises. Good ones. Anyway, give me your phone."

With hand extended palm up, she wiggled her delicate fingers. He handed it over and she entered her number, then texted herself.

"There. Now I'll know it's you."

When she handed his phone back, her soft fingers accidentally brushed his, sending a shockwave up his arm. He held back a growl. What was wrong with him? Hadn't Janessa been proof enough that he couldn't trust women? That he would be a bachelor for life?

"Dalton? Is there someplace I can get lunch? I'm still on eastern time and I think I missed a meal."

Blasted heat spread across his face again. He should have asked if she had eaten.

"I can drive you over to the dining hall if you'd like. Our coffee shop serves baked goods, breakfast, and lunch sandwiches until five."

"Perfect."

She grabbed a backpack and her purse. He held the front door open as she brushed past him. Her sweet fragrance sent his pulse thrumming again. It was going to be a long six weeks.

Once he dropped her off, he drove over to the ranch house, aware of how his day had gotten away from him. When he entered the six-thousand square-foot house, a chime sounded.

"Dalton, is that you?" Mami called from the kitchen.

He ambled toward the kitchen. When he entered, Mami frowned.

"¡Qué oso! Tell me you did not pick up River Sloane looking like that!"

Dalton glanced down and saw a dark streak on his sleeve. Mami shook her head and wagged a finger at him before dropping her hand at her waist.

"Don't worry, Mami. I didn't embarrass myself." At least not with the state of his shirt. "I had to fix her sink."

"I will have to take it to the cleaners. Hector's niece will know how to get—" Mami waved her finger in a circle. "That out."

"Gracias, Mamita."

"Was she bonita?"

Dalton frowned. She was more than just pretty. She was gorgeous and amazing. But he wasn't about to admit it to his match-making mother.

He shrugged. "How would I know?"

Then he turned on his heel and marched to his room. His hand shook slightly as he unbuttoned his soiled shirt. Quickly, he changed into a snap front work shirt and rugged, work jeans before he stowed his fancy boots in his closet. He retrieved the worn and scuffed brown boots, sliding them onto his socked feet. Like a glove.

After swapping to his dusty ranch hat, he walked to the far end of the enormous house to his office. Then he sighed at the stack of paperwork. Feeling too antsy, he decided physical labor suited his mood better.

"Mami!" he hollered toward the kitchen.

She stuck her head around the doorway. "Si, mijo?"

"I'm headed out again."

"Si. Tell your brothers they should eat at the dining hall tonight. No *cena familiar* tonight."

He frowned. Typically, family dinners were Wednesdays and Sundays. No family dinner on a Wednesday was odd.

"Is everything okay?"

"Si. Tres is taking me on a date tonight."

Dalton smiled. "Have fun with Papi."

"Tell River I look forward to meeting her tomorrow."

He nodded and left the house, texting his brothers as he strode to his truck.

A few hours later, he returned home to shower. After laboring in the blistering sun fixing a fence, he smelled like a boys' locker room. The last thing he wanted to do was send River running, if she was at the dining hall. Once in fresh clothes, he grabbed his cologne and spritzed it on without thinking. Why had he done that? His brothers would tease him for sure.

As he drove over to the dining hall, he wondered how River had spent her afternoon. Then he let out a frustrated sigh. He had no business thinking about the pretty romance author. She was here for six weeks before she went back to wherever she came from. No point in setting himself up for heartache. He needed to forget about her and those stunning hazel eyes and silky blond hair.

3

AFTER DALTON DROPPED her off at the dining hall, River explored the building. Large log beams spanned the expanse of the ceiling. Distressed yellowish-ivory paint covered the walls. Rough hewn wood floors ran the length of the space. Pottery, frames, and tapestries decorated the walls, with wrought iron crosses and sconces in between. The decor transported her back to the 1950s southwest. Classic dude ranch era. Probably their intent.

A verse above the exterior double doors caught her attention.

With regard to the works of man, by the word of your lips I have avoided the ways of the violent. My steps have held fast to your paths; my feet have not slipped. Psalms 17:4-5.

Underneath the verses was a sentence with a brand in the middle of it. The brand had an uppercase "V" in the center, with a lowercase "d" on one side and an "8" on the other.

D. V. 8. Oh! Deviate.

She read the full sentence: I do not dV8 from the Lord's plan.

Huh. Pretty bold to post scripture and an obvious Christian motto in the dining hall. Yet, she liked it and it spoke to her troubled heart.

"I do not deviate from the Lord's plan," she whispered.

"I see you figured out the family motto."

A tenor voice behind her startled her. River turned toward a much younger Vargas brother. She remembered seeing him in the photo online, too. A black t-shirt stretched across his broad shoulders, though narrower than Dalton's. Tattoos covered his exposed arms. A black and white pinstriped apron hid his waist, but she still noticed the rugged denim on his legs and black cowboy boots on his feet. He had pulled his long black hair back into a man-bun on the top of his head. A closely trimmed beard covered his jawline, and a mustache topped his lip, which stretched into a friendly smile. His dark brown eyes sparkled.

"You must be the romance author. Drake Vargas, youngest of the Vargas brothers. And your friendly cowboy barista."

He extended his hand, and she shook it as she introduced herself.

"Care for some coffee?" he asked as he rounded the coffee counter.

"Please. I'm suffering from serious jet lag right now."

"Where are you from?" he asked after he shut off the coffee grinder.

"Columbus, Ohio." Her stomach chose that moment to growl loudly.

"Hungry? We won't serve dinner for a few hours yet."

"I think I missed lunch completely. I'll take…" She perused the snacks in the display case. "A brownie and string cheese."

Drake laughed, a hearty sound that echoed in the deserted room. "One string cheese and brownie coming right up. Want me to warm the brownie?"

"Oh, that sounds delightful!"

He handed her the cheese. She tore off the plastic wrapper. Then she pulled the cheese apart, letting the salty string curl on her tongue.

"Cholla Casita, right?"

River nodded. "Must be slow if you know who is in

what room."

He tapped several times on the point-of-sale tablet before he said, "Mami made everyone promise to take care of her favorite romance author. Find a seat. I'll bring your order to you."

River chose a seat near the window with a view of the mountains. The aroma of fresh ground espresso filled the air as she tore off another stringy piece of cheese. She chewed and swallowed it. The bright blue sky complemented the browns and reds of Dalton Peak. A sense of contentment and joy filled her heart as she studied the beautiful scenery. She took a deep breath, feeling fully present in the moment.

A few minutes later, Drake set the coffee and brownie in front of her.

She slurped from the straw, savoring the best mocha she had ever tasted. "This is delicious."

"Can I get you anything else?"

"Do you have wifi?"

"Of course. The sign over there has the wifi name and password."

"Thanks."

Drake let her know he would be around the dining hall if she needed anything else.

River retrieved her e-ink tablet from her backpack and turned it on. She loved the device. It was a distraction-free electronic notepad that she had splurged on a few months ago. She already had several notebooks with ideas for novels, characters, and settings. Unfortunately, all of them would sit on the shelf for a while. Especially if she was gonna write a cowboy romance.

She sighed and ripped off a chunk of brownie. The sweet, gooey chocolate goodness made her feel better instantly. Chocolate was her best friend.

She tapped on her tablet and created a new notebook named "Cowboy Romance." Her stomach knotted as she let her gaze travel to the scenic mountain outside.

Dalton Peak. She chuckled, still amused by the name. She reeled her thoughts in before she dwelled on the handsome cowboy.

Instead, she mulled over the situation that brought her there. As worry rose again, she turned it into prayers.

Lord, please help me. I'm at a precipice. A crossroad. I must change and adapt, but a part of me wants to stay the same. I love writing workplace romances. The ideas come when I least expect it. But cowboys? I don't know the first thing about them. Or ranches. Or the West.

River ate another bite of brownie. Closing her eyes, she breathed deeply. An image of Dalton Vargas came to mind. Dressed in his fancy cowboy suit. Shining gold eyes. Chiseled features. The red that had covered his neck and face when she caught him watching her. The empty ring finger announcing his single status. Hmmm. He was a very handsome man.

Slowly, she opened her eyes and fanned her face before polishing off the brownie.

That. That was what readers wanted. A handsome, chivalrous, kind cowboy. The perfect picture of manliness and Americana. An icon that harkened back to a time where men were manly and family values meant something. Not the baffling world view screaming at them all day, every day, demoralizing their very soul—her very soul.

She quickly scrawled the words from her mind onto the tablet. This would be the theme to anchor her in the unfamiliar subgenre. If she accepted it, her new mission was to bring stories with strong family values to worn out women. Stories that boasted men as God designed them to be. Strong. Courageous. Yet, submitted to their Lord and Savior—exhibiting the love of Christ in their interactions with those around them. Family. Faith. Freedom in Christ.

Thank you, God, for encouraging me and for defining my purpose.

River moved her head in circles, wondering how long

she had sat there. The spicy aroma of Mexican food wafted around her. She stood, groaning at the stiffness in her legs. After stretching her arms over her head, she pushed in her chair. She placed the empty brownie plate on the shelf above the trash and tossed her empty cup before walking back to her seat.

A throat cleared behind her, so she turned and met the gaze of a very tall cowboy who occupied too many of her thoughts already. His spicy cologne was like a shot of adrenaline, making her heart race with anticipation.

"Would you like to join the family for dinner?" Dalton asked as he motioned toward a long table that seated ten.

"Sure." River stuffed her things into her backpack and dropped it on a chair.

Dalton's hand hovered behind the small of her back, guiding her toward the buffet line without touching her. The kind gesture made her feel special. Important. She would make a note of that later and use it in her book. Once in line, he handed her a plate.

She stared at the unfamiliar food. The only Mexican food she had eaten was tacos and fajitas. Nachos too.

"What are—" She glanced at the card in front of a tray of something that looked liked steamed corn husks.

"Tamales? You should try one."

"What is it?"

Dalton laughed. "Only one of the best things you'll ever eat."

"Are they spicy?" The last thing she needed was an IBS flare on her first night.

"No. They aren't. The meat has some seasoning, similar to taco seasoning. Authentic taco seasoning. I think the filling is cornmeal and ground beef. Ask Renata. She'll know."

River took one and moved down the line to something in a reddish brown sauce. The heavy spicy smell made her leery.

"Enchiladas in a mole sauce. It's spicy, but not too hot.

Try some."

She took one of each dish and resolved to eat at least one bite. Dalton explained what each one was as they made their way to the end of the line.

"Just wait for dessert. Empanadas are the best."

"They aren't spicy, are they?"

Dalton chuckled, a rich sound that brought a smile to her face. "I take it you're not a fan of spicy food."

"Let's just say it's not a fan of me."

"Gotcha. The empanadas are sweet with a touch of cinnamon and honey. You'll like them, I promise."

After he set his plate at the head of the table, Dalton remained standing. River placed her plate on the table and followed his lead. Each brother and the two women from the office did the same. Then Dalton reached for his brother's hand to his left and her hand to his right. Warmth traveled up her arm from the gentle touch all the way to her heart as she bowed her head.

Dalton's loud voice carried throughout the dining hall. His humility was evident, even in his commanding presence.

"Lord Jesus. We thank you for blessing us with this ranch and new guests to come enjoy the wonder of Your majestic creation. Please be with Mateo. Help his hand heal quickly. Watch over Mami and Papi on their date. Continue to ease Padre's pain. We look forward to dining with him soon. And thank you, Lord, for bringing River Sloane to share a meal with us. Bless this food and may our words and actions reflect You."

All the men and women around her raised their voices. "We do not deviate from Your plan. Amen."

The hair on her arms stood on end. She could *feel* the Lord's presence—something she had only experienced a handful of times. A welcome peace wrapped her body like a cloak. God was with her in this next stage of her career. Somehow, she knew she would be okay.

Dalton held her chair while two of his brothers did the

same for the other women. Once the three women were seated, the men sat down. She had seen nothing like it before. It touched her deeply, stirring something she didn't have the time to explore right then.

One thing was certain, this trip to nowhere Arizona had God's fingerprints all over it.

As DALTON TOOK a seat, he noticed a shift in River's demeanor. She went quiet and sipped her iced tea. He wondered what had upset her.

"Everything okay?"

She nodded, and a faint smile graced her pink lips. "I think it will be. Yes."

He held her gaze for a few seconds longer until her eyes darted to her food.

"Tamales, huh?"

When River's fork hovered over the tamale, husk still intact, he quietly peeled back the husk on his own.

Her pretty eyes rounded. "Oh! So, you don't eat that part."

He flashed her a smile with a quick shake of his head. He couldn't tear his eyes away from her as she took her first bite of tamale. When her eyes lit with pleasure, he was glad he had slowed down to notice. The second bite elicited a similar reaction.

"This is phenomenal!"

Dalton laughed. Derin slapped him on the shoulder, causing his jovial mood to dim.

"Got a gringo in the house," Derin teased. He winked at River and her cheeks flushed.

Dalton narrowed his eyes at his flirtatious, outgoing brother. Others considered them gringos too, if not for their mother's Mexican heritage. Of all the brothers, only Drake kind of looked like their mother.

"I'm Derin, by the way."

"Nice to meet you," River replied.

When Drake responded next, Dalton relaxed. "Yeah, he's the loud-mouth attention hog. You'd never guess he's a middle child."

"Watch out, *mija*."

Drake growled. *"Mijo."*

"You know they do that just to irritate you," Renata said.

Derin raised his voice an octave and batted his lashes. "Mamacita's boy."

Dalton turned toward his obnoxious brother. *"Chitón."*

River angled toward Dylan, who sat on her other side. After she asked his name, she asked, *"Mija? Mijo?* What are you saying?"

Dylan's face turned bright red. No surprise there. He barely spoke to horses, much less people. In fact, Dalton wondered why he sat next to River. Surely he knew their guest would want to engage in conversation.

Solana answered, "'Mija' is an affectionate way to say 'my daughter'. 'Mijo' is the same, but for a son. And Dalton told him to shut up, or more accurately, to shush."

"Yeah, they like to tease Drake about being a Mama's boy," Renata said. "Aunt Catalina hovers."

"Just because I have asthma and every dust storm could end me, doesn't mean I'm a mama's boy."

"Don't be so dramatic," Devon piped up, rolling his eyes.

River smiled. "When do I get to meet all the other Dalton J. Vargases? And how many are there again?"

Devon cleared his throat.

"Oh, boy. Here it comes," Drake said. "Devon is our resident historian. Not officially. He just loves history, including family history."

"Someone has to pass down information from generation to generation," Devon defended.

Dalton reached for the sriracha and liberally shook it over his tamale. Unlike River, he enjoyed the heat.

"Dalton J. Vargas, Sr., was our great-grandpa. He married a lovely Mexican woman named Maria. Their firstborn son, Dalton J. Vargas, Jr., was four years old when they started this place in 1952."

"Wow. It's that old?"

Devon nodded. "Junior is our grandpa, who we fondly call Padre. He also married a Mexican woman. Her name was Elena."

"So beautiful," River said, wistfully, as her eyes softened.

A strange sensation overcame Dalton, and he felt a tug in the depths of his heart. He had always wanted to pay homage to their grandmother by naming his future daughter after her. He frowned and forced the thought away. Janessa had made sure he would never risk his heart again. Maybe he would have a niece with that name someday.

"Their firstborn was Dalton J. Vargas, the third who goes by Tres, our Papi. His brother, Diego Vargas, is our uncle and Renata and Solana's father. He lives in town and runs the feed store with his wife, Kate."

"And your mother, Catalina. Is she Mexican?" River asked.

"Yes," Devon answered.

When River met his gaze, Dalton chewed slower. A gnawing stirred in his gut as his hand tightened around the cold metal of his fork.

"So, it sounds like Dalton J. Vargas the fourth needs to marry a Mexican woman and their firstborn son already has a name: Dalton J. Vargas the fifth."

Even her wink did little to stop the icy chill sliding down his spine. He swallowed as the table went silent.

"I'm the last of the Dalton Vargases." His heart hammered in his chest, hoping she would leave off it.

"Well," River laughed. "That doesn't seem fair. After all, don't you want your son growing up thinking an entire mountain was named after him?"

His brothers and cousins roared. A smile even twitched at the corner of his own mouth against his will. She had a good sense of humor. Too bad it was on a topic that brought him so much pain.

Derin said, "D4 here has sworn off women. Plans to be a bachelor forever."

Dylan leaned closer to River and muttered, "Janessa wrecked him."

"Enough!" Dalton yelled, pounding his fist on the table, which caused the silverware to jump and clatter.

His family stilled, their eyes widening in surprise. The sudden hush that fell over the room was deafening.

Anger coursed through him. He launched to his feet, grabbing his plastic glass, and stormed over to the soda fountain. Curse his brothers for bringing up Janessa. It still felt too raw. Even after three years. Why did they have to bring it up in front of River?

He punched the button for a Coke and waited for the dark fizzy beverage to fill his glass. The smell of syrup made him crave it more.

"Hey." Dylan's soft voice came from behind him. "They're just teasing you."

Dalton swiveled to face him, cracking his neck from side to side. The motion did little to soothe his rage.

Dylan pressed one glass against the ice dispenser, then another. He filled the first with iced tea and the second with Coke.

"I think you hurt her feelings," Dylan, his brother who could barely string together a sentence in front of a woman, said.

Dalton flicked his gaze to her. Her shoulders slumped forward and the smile in her eyes had dimmed as she listened to whatever story Derin was telling.

Crud. Dylan was right. He let out a loud breath, raking a hand through his short hair.

"That's better," Dylan said before walking back to the table.

Dalton hung out by the soda fountain for another minute, watching as Dylan handed the iced tea to River and took his seat. So much for not embarrassing himself again. He ambled toward his chair and eased into it. When he dared to look at River, she mouthed the words, "I'm sorry."

He tried to smile but knew it came across strained.

"Does the family surname originate in Mexico?" River asked.

"No," Devon responded, while Dalton cringed. They were still on that subject?

"It's Spanish in origin. Many of our ancestors came from a long line of wealthy Spaniards that migrated west over the years. Best I could figure, our Mexican heritage comes from the women in our family line."

Derin made a fake snoring sound. "Boring. River, tell us about yourself."

Dalton hid his sigh behind a swig of soda. At last, something he wanted to hear more about.

"Um. What would you like to know?"

Renata grinned. "Only everything! When did you write your first novel? What are you working on now? Are any of your stories based—"

"Whoa, Rennie, give the woman a chance to respond," Derin interjected.

Dalton noticed the frown that flashed across River's face.

"You don't have to answer the invasive questions," he whispered.

"How about I tell you a little about my family since I just grilled you on yours?"

Renata nodded vehemently.

"I'm an only child. My grandparents were hippies in the '70s. They roamed all over the country. Slept in VW vans and all the stereotypes about hippies were true of them."

"Is that why your parents named you River?" Solana asked.

Dalton breathed easier when River laughed. "No. That's why my mother is named Sunflower, though she goes by Sunny. And she's about what you'd expect from hippie parents. Artsy. Into crystals and metaphysical stuff."

A stab of guilt hit his chest. Maybe his prayer had made her uncomfortable earlier, only she had been too polite to say anything. Still, he wouldn't be living up to the family motto if he failed to pray over a meal.

"I take it you aren't?" Renata asked.

"No. I believe the Bible is God's Word and a guide for how we are to live our lives. Very different ideals from either of my parents."

Ah, so she was a Christian. Interesting. Dalton wondered how and when that happened, given her upbringing.

"Anyway, my name comes from Dr. Who."

Blank stares looked her way. He did not know what that was, either.

"The SciFi TV show?"

They all shook their heads.

Dalton cleared his throat. "We don't have a TV. Never have."

Her eyes rounded so big he thought they might pop out of their sockets.

"No TVs? Ever?"

He chuckled. "Correct."

"Not exactly," Derin said. "We watched sports in the bunkhouse when our old foreman, Mateo, snuck us in."

Dalton clamped his jaw shut.

"Oh, you definitely won't understand the reference to my name. The short version is there is a character named River Song on the show. Guess she appeared in some books long before the show aired, because my dad, a huge SciFi fan, convinced my mother it was the perfect name. River

Sloane. Mom loved it and thought it sounded appropriate for the granddaughter of hippies."

Dalton studied River as she shared a few funny stories about her opposites-attract parents. She relayed the details in a way that made seemingly mundane stories come to life. He could envision her childhood home. Her mother sounded sweet, but a little spacey. Her dad sounded a lot like him—serious and practical.

Drake excused himself and headed to the kitchen. A few minutes later, he brought out a tray.

"Who wants empanadas?" Drake asked, effectively ending the family history conversation.

Dalton took a bite of his empanada and savored the sweetness. Chef's were as good as Mami's.

His gaze shifted to River. When her eyes fluttered closed, her dark lashes fanning her cheeks, he knew she enjoyed that first bite. A cute hum rose from her throat as her eyelids revealed excited hazel eyes. He could get lost in those.

"These are so good!"

His mouth went dry when she licked the honey from her lips. He shoved the last bite of his empanada in his mouth.

There was nothing ordinary about River Sloane. Despite the mountain of paperwork waiting for him at home, he lingered, listening to her talk.

She asked him questions about the ranch after everyone else left. She told him more about her life back in Ohio. He didn't want to leave.

As dusk fell, Dalton offered to drive River back to her casita. When she declined, saying she wanted to explore the property, he puzzled over why that left him disappointed.

4

THE NEXT MORNING, River groaned as the first rays of sunlight filtered in through the window. She swiped the alarm on her phone to silence it. Then she dug a pair of jean shorts and a fitted t-shirt from the dresser, showered, and hurried across the common area to the dining hall. She glanced at her watch. Five-thirty. She didn't get up that early back home. Normally she rolled out of bed around eight. Sometimes later, if she stayed up late to write.

"Morning, River!" Drake greeted her as she entered. "Iced mocha this morning?"

"Bless you. Make it a triple shot, please."

"Better get some breakfast. Dalton won't wait around for you much longer."

Much longer? Renata told her to meet him at the dining hall at five-thirty.

When Drake handed her the coffee, she sucked down several gulps from the straw with her eyes closed. The sweet, caffeinated beverage gave her the jolt she needed.

"You are a miracle worker, Drake. Thank you."

She opened her eyes to a scowling Dalton.

"Uh, oh," Drake said before he busied himself wiping down the counters.

"Where are your jeans?"

River blinked at him. Why did she need jeans? Wasn't it supposed to be a million degrees out that day?

"And boots?"

"Um. It's hot. I only brought shorts. And I'm not a cow-girl, so why would I have boots?"

Dalton closed his eyes, groaning. "Renata!"

"Yes, boss," she said as she skidded to a stop in front of him.

"Get her some clothes."

"I have clothes," River said to his retreating back.

He waved an arm in the air as he shoved the double doors open. They creaked in protest before slamming shut.

"Sorry about that," Renata said. "None of us realized you might not know what to wear to work on the ranch. Your company didn't give us much to go on when they made the arrangements."

River's stomach knotted. She hadn't even started her second day, and she had already ticked off the handsome cowboy. The one she thoroughly enjoyed getting to know after dinner last night.

Renata's face softened. "Don't worry. You look about my size, maybe a little thinner. And shorter. Still…"

She looped her arm around River's and tugged. Her smile was sympathetic.

"It'll be fine. We'll take care of you."

She hopped in Renata's white Jeep and held on as the young woman sped over bumps in the dirt road as if they didn't exist. They did. River's jarring teeth attested to it. When Renata slammed on the brakes by a plain stucco building, the tires skidded, and the vehicle angled slightly to the right in the parking space.

"Come on."

River grabbed her coffee and sipped it as she followed Renata into the building.

"What size shoe do you wear?"

"Eight."

"Hmm. We may have to see if Aunt Catalina has a pair of boots you can borrow. Mine will be too big, and the last thing you need is blisters."

Renata breezed through the apartment at a clip. River half jogged to keep up.

At last she slowed in front of a closet and dresser. She tossed two pairs of jeans on the edge of her bed. Then she grabbed a bright pink long-sleeved top.

"Try these on."

"Long sleeves?" River asked, cringing. Sweat would drench her in an hour.

"It's heavy enough to protect your skin from the sun and… Other things. But it's breathable so you won't pass out from the heat. Promise."

Other things? River wasn't sure she wanted to know, so she didn't ask.

Renata closed the door behind her. River quickly stripped down and donned the first pair of jeans. They were kind of baggy on her, but with a belt they might be okay. The bright pink shirt actually looked good on her. It was more comfortable than she thought. After slipping her tennis shoes on again, she entered the living room.

"Don't suppose you have a belt?"

"One sec."

Renata returned with one, and once River threaded it through the belt loops, the jeans stayed put.

"I'll bring by another outfit and leave it in your room. On Saturday, we can make a trip to town and you can pick out things you want. Oh! A hat. I'll meet you in the Jeep."

Once Renata joined her, River took the offered hat and placed it on her head. Nice.

"Here's a ponytail holder. You'll want to braid your hair to keep it out of your way."

River quickly braided it and flung the thick braid over her shoulder as Renata pulled up to a ranch house. This must be the family's home.

The massive single-story home looked similar to her casita. Touches of wood logs complemented the tan stucco exterior. A sweeping porch spanned the entire length of the house. Several groupings of cushioned patio chairs provided the perfect view of the desert and Dalton Peak. River could imagine the view at sunset.

Renata's voice stirred her from her thoughts.

"Oh, good. Dalton's truck is here. He can take you over to the stables. I've gotta run. Just go on in. I'm sure Catalina will be in the kitchen. She can help you find boots that fit."

River hopped out of the Jeep. A cloud of dust billowed in Renata's wake as she drove away.

Just walk on in, huh?

She swallowed down a lump in her throat and pushed the fancy wood door open. A chime sounded.

"Rennie, is that you?" A woman's voice sounded from somewhere deep within the house.

River stood, mouth agape, as she took in the immense living room. The ceiling had to be at least thirty feet tall. Round log beams, similar to the ones in her casita, ran the length of the room, only much larger in scale. A glossy end table made from the cross section of a massive tree stood next to each piece of comfortable leather furniture. Just like everywhere else, brightly colored frames, tapestries, and decor brought vibrancy to the room. Floor to ceiling windows flooded it with natural light. The bank of windows shared the same spectacular view as the porch.

"Oh, River!"

A short Mexican woman shuffled toward her, arms extended. She engulfed River in a warm embrace. "I'm so glad to meet you. Have my sons and nieces treated you *muy bien*?"

River shook off her awe of the amazing space and offered the kind woman a smile.

"Yes. Everyone has been nice."

"What brings you up to the house?"

River pointed to her feet. "Renata said you could hook me up with some boots. Guess I didn't pack appropriately for ranch work."

"*Dios mio*! No, those sneakers won't do. Come."

Catalina clasped her arm, half dragging her to the far reaches of the house into a bedroom as large as River's entire apartment back in Columbus.

She told Catalina her size. The sweet woman ruffled through the bottom of the closet and produced two different pairs of boots. River tried them both on and settled on the warm brown ones.

"You can keep those. They were a little big for me and I never wore them."

"Really? Let me at least pay for them."

"Oh, no. My gift to you."

River shrugged, not sure what would come next.

"We must get you to Dalton. Knowing my son, he's probably irritated by the delay. That boy loves his schedules. Sometimes so much he forgets how to stop and enjoy life."

"Mami!" Dalton frowned at his mother when they met him in the living room. "Don't tell her all my secrets."

When he leaned down and presented his cheek to his mother, River's heart fluttered. Catalina kissed his cheek, and he grinned. Something about a man who loved his mama. Got to her every time. In real life and in her novels.

"*Vamos!*" his mother said, waving her hands toward the door.

River let out a loud breath when she climbed onto the seat of his truck. What a whirlwind morning!

"So, what's first?"

Dalton cleared his throat. "Your company said to put you to work. Are you sure you want to?"

River tried to muster a cheery tone. "I'm here to learn about cowboys and ranching, so… Whatever it takes to help me write a better story."

"Just tell me if we work you too hard."

"I'm all yours, boss."

His head swiveled toward her, and his gaze locked with

hers, stealing her breath away. His eyes, like a turbulent sea, held both mystery and a glimmer of hope. Under his unwavering gaze, her throat went dry. He finally broke eye contact and backed his manly truck out of the parking space.

"Get ready for some sore muscles, Miss River Sloane. 'Cause cowboys and cowgirls are very hard workers."

"Even the Ranch Manager?" she teased, hoping to ease the tightening in her stomach.

"Especially the Ranch Manager."

Once at the stables, River donned a pair of work gloves and took the shovel Dalton thrust toward her. As he explained how to muck a stall, the sweet smell of hay tickled her nose.

She shoveled horse poo—ew—into a wheelbarrow. Some of it got on her shirtsleeve. Must be one of those "other things" her long sleeves protected her from. Just how much poo could one horse produce?

Sweat trickled down her back, making her t-shirt stick to her skin underneath the borrowed snap front shirt. Wicking t-shirts and tanks went on her mental list of clothing to buy.

When she glanced over at Dalton, his penetrating gaze made her second-guess her efforts. Nervously, she asked if she was doing it right. He told her she was, so she continued with the manual labor, her arms already sore.

Though tempted to complain, River reminded herself this dirty research might just resurrect her career.

DALTON THOUGHT RIVER looked stunning in her sundress yesterday. But in jeans and a snap front shirt? She looked downright sexy. Renata's choice of bright pink made River's face glow.

As she scraped the shovel in the stall, his gaze raked over her figure. Yeah, teaching her ranch work was a bad idea. He ought to assign Derin the task. The thought of his charming brother spending hours alone with River made him feel sick to his stomach.

Maybe Devon would be a better choice. He would probably bore her to tears recounting every historical fact he could think of about the ranch, Wickenburg, and even Arizona. Then again, River was a writer. She might geek out on history, too. That's the last thing he needed. One of his brothers falling for her.

And just why did that bother him so much?

"Like this?" she asked as she carried the full shovel to the manure wheelbarrow.

"I'd give you a B minus. Not bad for your first stall."

Once she dumped the contents of the shovel, she flashed fierce hazel eyes in his direction.

"Challenge accepted. You do not know how competitive I am."

Probably not as competitive as five brothers on a ranch. Though he enjoyed bringing it out in her.

"Can I leave you to it, then?"

"Why? Where are you going?"

"I need to drive out to the construction site. Dylan is around here somewhere. If you need anything, just text me or Renata."

When River leaned against the shovel handle, she removed the borrowed cowboy hat and swiped the back of a gloved hand across her forehead. "Is it always this hot?"

"It's worse before a storm, when the humidity spikes."

"Great." She groaned as her body sagged against the wall.

"Remember to drink lots of water. There's a fridge with chilled bottles in the tack room. Drink more than you usually would at home. Don't want any trips to the hospital for dehydration."

Her pretty eyes widened, and he chuckled.

"Not to worry. I'm teasing. But not about the water.

Drink every time you take a break."

"How many stalls do I need to clean?"

"All of them."

She blew out a loud breath. "You have some ibuprofen somewhere, right?"

"And a jacuzzi by the pool. You'll probably want to take a dip in it this evening."

She nodded.

"You brought a swimsuit, right?" Heat spread over his face as he pictured what she might look like in one.

"Two, actually."

He pivoted and headed out to his truck before he made a pithy comment he would regret. Just thinking about her in a swimsuit had his pulse jetting.

Focus, Dalton. She was a guest. Here today and gone in a few weeks.

The rest of the day, he split his time between the tennis court construction site and on the UTV, driving the perimeter. Monsoon storms would arrive any day. He needed to see with his own eyes that any sources of fuel for a brush fire had been removed. Not that he didn't trust his men. There was too much at stake, not to be certain. One lightning strike igniting dead brush could spread through the ranch swiftly. If it happened, it could set them back for years.

His phone buzzed in his shirt pocket. He stopped the UTV and looked at it.

Renata had texted: *We're all meeting at the dining hall. River too. Hot tub after.*

He pointed the UTV toward the equipment barn. As soon as he arrived at the barn, a cowboy offered to take care of the UTV.

Dalton tossed a *gracias* over his shoulder as he jogged to his truck. He sniffed the edge of his shirt. He needed a shower, which he barely had time for.

When he parked in front of the ranch house, he darted around to the back entrance, closer to his room. As he hurried down the hall, he stripped off his shirt. Once in the privacy of his bathroom, he quickly showered, running his hair under the warm spray. His muscles begged him to dally, but he didn't want to miss a dinner with River.

Again, he spritzed on cologne. He told himself it meant nothing. He wasn't trying to impress River. Or maybe...

Dalton shook off the thought and stuffed his feet into some athletic sandals. Good enough for dinner and the hot tub.

When he parked near the dining hall, he saw River walking with Renata and Solana. She wore a bright yellow dress with little blue flowers. The thin straps left her shoulders exposed. He noticed the swish of her skirt as she entered the dining room. He swallowed a few times, trying to bring back moisture to his dry throat.

After a second to calm his racing pulse, he left the quiet of his truck and joined the others inside. Loud voices and the clank of silverware hitting plates assaulted his ears. River sat at the table with a full plate of food. She smiled when she noticed him, sending his heart rate ticking up again.

As Dalton made his way through the line, he chastised himself. He needed to control his attraction to the beautiful romance author. In a few weeks, she would be gone, back to Ohio. The last thing he needed was a broken heart.

Dalton took a seat across from River, thankful someone had left it open. That train of thought wouldn't help him.

Derin told a story about the calving season and River listened closely. A twinge of jealousy tightened Dalton's gut. He wanted her to look at him with rapt attention. Not his more charming younger brother.

As he swallowed a bite of his food, he mentally kicked himself. Two things he knew for certain. First, no woman would ever choose him over Derin. Many single women guests preferred his brother's broad shoulders, flirty personality, and charisma. The last woman on Derin's arm had been a cougar.

Second, Dalton really must stop thinking about River. After Janessa, he had no desire to end up crushed by a woman again. He had too much on his plate, anyway.

Once Dalton finished his meal, Renata asked if he was going with them to the pool. He froze, thinking about the stack of paperwork waiting for him in his office. His gaze snagged on River's hopeful expression and before he knew it, he agreed. So he guided River to the hot tub.

When he looked around the pool area, no one else came. His cousin's trickery didn't fool him. She had set him up.

Sighing, he turned his back and removed his t-shirt.

He heard River's soft gasp. At first, it brought a smile to his face. Then he remembered the unsightly scar. He always forgot about it since it was on his back.

"What happened?" she asked softly.

As he turned to face her, his throat went dry. Even though her one-piece suit was modest, it still sent his heart pounding against his chest. Any minute now, he expected to have to lasso it back. There was no way he was going to survive six weeks with this woman and not face some collateral damage.

5

RIVER'S BREATH CAUGHT when she noticed Dalton's incredibly contoured back. Then she gasped as her eyes landed on a three-inch puckered scar on the right, slightly above his waistline. She asked him about it as she piled her hair into a knot on the top of her head.

When he turned to face her, any remaining breath left her lungs. The cowboy had muscles defined enough to send any woman's heart racing. Hers certainly galloped. She forced herself to look away as she gingerly stepped into the hot tub.

Dalton twisted a dial and bubbles belched from the jets, creating a frothy foam layer on the water. Good. Maybe she would stop staring at his torso once the water hid those muscles beneath the surface. She wrinkled her nose at the overwhelming smell of chlorine in the air.

"The scar?" she asked again.

He grunted. "I forget it's there. That happened a long time ago. I was only twelve or thirteen, I think."

River leaned into one powerful jet stream, letting it pound against her sore shoulder, loosening the tension. Then she shifted to the other before settling away from the pressurized water.

"One afternoon, I had been riding to catch up with Papi. Must have been the summer or a weekend. I don't rightly recall. Anyway, I spotted a calf on the other side of the barbed wire fence. I knew how important even a single calf was. So, instead of riding to fetch my dad or another adult, I figured I could get the calf back in the fence all on my own."

"Dalt, you didn't?" Goodness. She had just given him a nickname. What was wrong with her? Heat warmed her entire face.

His mouth hung open for a second before he continued.

"I grabbed my gloves from my saddlebags and dismounted my horse. Then I looked around for something to prop open the fence. I had watched my dad and uncle do something similar a few years before, not knowing how foolish it was to try it on my own."

River waited with bated breath.

"I made it through to the other side, no problem. Then I lassoed the calf and led it back through the opening. Right about the time I felt proud of myself, the calf kicked backward, knocking away the wood stick. The barbed wire collapsed onto my back and chewed my skin. Even though I knew better, I panicked and squirmed, sending it deeper into my flesh."

She pictured the scene. Hot sun beat down on his back. A young teen wanted to make his father proud. Took on more responsibility than he ought. Things went awry and the almost man showed his young age. Acted like a frightened teen. Piercing pain radiated from the puncture wound.

Moisture gathered in the corners of her eyes. She stretched out her arm and placed her hand on his forearm, which casually rested on the hot tub edge. His arm twitched beneath her fingertips, though his gaze remained fixed on an unseen point in time.

"After trying to free myself and failing, I finally let my body slacken. The wire bit and burned. Blood soaked my shirt. I hung there at an awkward angle, suspended several inches above the ground. Two hours later, my father found me."

Dalton's eyes locked on hers now. Breathing became

more difficult.

"It's the only time in my life I remember seeing fear in his eyes."

As the sun lowered in the sky behind the mountain, low voltage landscaping lights flickered on. The light in the bottom of the hot tub reflected in Dalton's gold eyes. River couldn't look away.

"He and my uncle snipped a section of the fence off to free me. Papi carried me draped over his lap on his horse, murmuring softly. Comforting words for me mixed with prayers to God. My vision blurred. It hurt so bad. I thought I was dying."

Finally, Dalton looked away and snorted. "Funny, the things that run through a boy's mind in a crisis."

"Anyway, the story told at family gatherings is that Papi sat in the back of his beat up old Ford truck, still cradling me on my stomach while Uncle Diego drove like the wind. I spent the night in the ER as doctors cut away some of my skin to remove the deeply embedded barbs. After many stitches and pumped full of fluids and painkillers, they sent me home."

Dalton's hand found hers as he continued the story, lacing his fingers with hers. She liked the feel of her small hand against his large, rough one.

"I was lucky, you know. Lucky they found me when they did. Lucky not to die from dehydration. Fortunate to live close to a hospital. There are so many other ways my story could have ended."

He cleared his throat. "Years later, I realized the 'what ifs' were why Papi had been so afraid. He understood that the desert reclaims its own. It could have reclaimed me."

"But for the grace of God," River whispered reverently.

"Exactly."

Silence settled over them. The churning water stilled, signaling the end of their hot tub time. Dalton loosened his hold on her hand and bounded out. Then he offered it to her as she climbed the stairs. At the side of the hot tub, the air between them ignited. Her heart raced even after he released her hand.

"I've told no one that story," he whispered as he took a step back.

River couldn't help herself. One corner of her mouth lifted into a half smile. "I don't suppose you run around the ranch with no shirt on all the time."

Her joke fell flat under the intensity of his gaze. He pivoted toward a nearby lounge chair and tossed her a beach towel emblazoned with the ranch's name and brand. She wrapped it around her body as she slid her feet into her flip-flops.

"Forgot to mention the plumber fixed the kitchenette sink. You should be good to go."

She let out a shaky breath, thankful for the change of subject to break the electricity sparking between them.

Dalton rubbed his towel over his chest and legs before he hung it around his shoulders.

"Feeling more relaxed?" he asked as he held the pool gate open for her.

"Much better. Maybe a little sleepy."

Dalton slid her hand in his again. She should pull hers away. She wasn't at Vargas Guest Ranch & Resort to fall in love. No, she had a job to do. Then she would fly home, leaving this magical place — this amazing man — behind.

"Ever ride a horse?" he asked as he swung their joined hands playfully.

"This might surprise you. Yes, I have. I spent a few summers on my hippie grandparents' farm, so I learned to ride there."

"Oh, so you already knew how to muck a stall?"

"Eh, not really. They hired help for that. As their only grandchild, they spoiled me when I visited."

Instead of turning toward the truck, he led her along the path to her casita. The slow pace matched the peacefulness settling in her soul. The heat radiating from the ground dried the remaining damp drops on her skin.

"Well, get some rest," he said as he stopped at her front porch.

As the silence stretched on, River's throat went dry and her palms grew sweaty. She cleared her throat and said, "Good night, Dalton."

"Night, River. Sweet dreams."

She placed the key card on the sensor and opened the door. He waved from the walkway before she closed it.

Sweet dreams indeed. She doubted she would sleep at all, dreaming about Dalton J. Vargas the fourth.

DALTON SCUFFED HIS feet on the pea gravel pathway. He was doing it again. Opening his heart to a woman. No good would come of it. He would only end up with scars deeper than the one on his back.

Other than light hair and hazel eyes, River shared nothing in common with Janessa. But he had only known her for two days. Hardly long enough to know anything at all. He wished he could get it through to his heart the dangerous game it played.

As he climbed into his truck, he slammed the door harder than he intended. A part of him wanted to pray and ask God not to allow him to fall in love. Then there was the hope as tiny as a mustard seed, dreaming that this time could be different.

What did he know? Nothing. That was what.

He backed up the truck and pointed it toward the ranch house, stopping near a horse corral used for staging trail rides. He cut the engine and lights. Then he opened the door and climbed into the truck bed. Leaning back, Dalton stared up at the speckling of stars across the sky.

A prayer danced at the corner of his mind and skittered away.

Janessa seemed nice at first, too. Flirty. Fun. Playful. She had teased him about being too serious and then made it her personal mission to loosen him up. She drew secrets from his heart like a magnet sweeping over hidden nails. He had no power to stop sharing his heart with her.

Their time together passed quickly. She had come vacationing with some girlfriends, who she quickly abandoned in favor of spending time with him. At the end of two weeks, he asked her if she could stay. She said she had nothing pressing back home — a place he had never asked about. After she supposedly adjusted her schedule, she stayed on. Moved into the women's housing. Started working in the office.

Renata tried to warn him about Janessa's dark side. Said the woman talked down to her and bossed her around, even though Renata knew more about the resort operations, despite her young age.

There were so many warnings he should have heeded. Instead, he let the pressure of his age — thirty-one at the time — and Mami's hopes for grandchildren influence his ignorance. He wanted to marry and have a family of his own. To fill his brother's old rooms with the next generation of Vargases. Have a daughter named Elena. Janessa convinced him she wanted the same things.

Renata said, after the fact, she thought Janessa may have been truly interested in him at first. But when she discovered how much money the resort alone earned in a year, and that he ran it all, her plans changed. Dollar signs became her motive. People were tools to be used toward that goal.

A deep ache pinched his heart. He rubbed a hand over it as the memories blurred his vision.

His proposal gave Janessa the confidence her plan had succeeded. Honestly, if he hadn't caught her flirting with a guest, he would have married her. When they broke up, she revealed her entire plan. She intended to get pregnant quickly, deliver the baby, divorce him, and take as much of his money as she could get her selfish hands on.

Yeah, Janessa wrecked him.

But for the grace of God.

River's words from earlier rolled around Dalton's mind.

Perhaps the breakup with Janessa had been God's grace, releasing him before her vitriol and disdain destroyed even more people.

Maybe River's presence was God's grace, too. A chance for genuine love.

Dalton discarded the thought as he jumped over the side of his truck and drove the rest of the way home.

Even if he risked his heart, he couldn't risk the ranch like that again. Three generations of Dalton J. Vargases came before him. Senior, Padre, and Papi had worked too hard to build the place. His legacy was to protect the ranch at all costs. The best way he could accomplish it was to remain single. Then no woman could steal what his family had built. They would pass it down to his brothers' children instead.

If this was the right answer, then why did it hurt so much?

Dalton sighed as he exited his truck and rounded to the back of the house. He eased the door open, hoping not to disturb anyone. Then he padded down the hallway to his suite, flicking the lights on.

"Mijo!"

He jumped at the sound of his mother's voice. He hadn't noticed her sitting on the edge of his bed as he entered his room.

"How was the pool?"

Dalton sighed as he kicked off his sandals.

Mami patted the spot next to her.

"My trunks are still wet." They weren't. He had spent plenty of time in the heat for them to dry completely.

"You forget, we have security cameras at the resort, no? You left hours ago."

"Mamacita, those cameras are for protection, not for spying on our guests."

"Ay. But they are good for spying on my sons."

She patted the corner of the bed again. Dalton trudged over to it and plopped down with a groan.

"She likes you."

"Mami—"

"*Chitón.* Let me speak."

Dalton angled so he could see her face.

"Mijo, you can have a life of your own. To fall in love."

When he grumbled, poised to remind her about Janessa, she held up a hand and he pursed his lips.

"Si. I know. Janessa." Mami rolled her eyes, rocking her head from side to side. "She was *mujer malvada.*"

He snorted. Evil woman described Janessa perfectly.

"Not all women are like her. Your mamacita is not, no?"

"No, Mami."

"Neither is River."

Dalton clenched his jaw tight. His gaze shifted to the corner of the room.

"It's okay to have dreams, mijo. To want a wife. A *familia.*"

"But the ranch—"

"Is a business. A piece of land."

"It's our livelihood, Mami. I could have destroyed it all." The guilt pressed heavily on his shoulders, twisting his gut.

"No. Do not believe lies. It is not your ranch any more than it is mine or Papi's. Our name is on it, but it is God's hands that direct it and protect it. If God wants it to end, it will end. If He wants it to continue, it will continue. Whether you are single or married. Have *niños* or not."

Mami pushed off the bed and opened her arms wide. Dalton stood, towering nearly a foot over her. He leaned down for her warm hug. As he broke the embrace, she reached up and placed a hand on his cheek, just like she had when he was a child.

"*Mi mijo.* Always trying to take on more responsibility than you should. Remember, we do not deviate from God's plan. But the plan it is God's, no? Not ours."

"Si, Mami."

"*Dulces sueños.*"

Dalton swallowed back the lump in his throat as his mother wished him sweet dreams and left. The same words he had said to River.

As he changed and climbed into bed, he prayed for peace. Mami's words of wisdom could wait until morning to take root.

6

On Saturday morning, River woke two minutes before her alarm. Even though most of the ranch employees put in a full day's work on Saturdays, Dalton gave River the day off. Kinda. He had assigned her to Renata for the day.

Renata had big plans for her, so she showered, donned shorts, a bright blue t-shirt, and her sneakers. After picking up a breakfast sandwich and coffee from the coffee shop, she met Renata in the office.

The reception area held similar rustic western decor as the dining hall. The smell of leather added to the cozy feel. Country music played softly in the background, creating a relaxed atmosphere. Yellow light emanated from lamps resting on end tables beside the leather chairs, casting a soft glow on the dark wood. Light wood-looking tile covered the floor, drawing her eyes deeper into the room. It felt like a warm and welcoming place, ready to embrace any visitors who stepped through the doors.

Solana welcomed her as the door swished closed behind her.

"Have you taken a proper tour of the property yet?" she asked.

"No. Dalton kept my days full on Thursday and Friday."

Renata entered the reception area from her office.

"Shall we start with a tour, then?"

"I would love to."

Renata led River outside to a golf cart. After River settled onto the warm tan leather seat, Renata backed out of the space.

"How was the hot tub the other night?" Renata asked.

River's face heated. "It definitely helped with my sore muscles."

"And Dalton?"

"You set it up, didn't you?"

Renata giggled. "Of course. Anyone with eyes can see he's taken with you. It's good to see him coming out of his shell. Maybe Janessa didn't damage him beyond repair."

River's pulse sped up. She quickly changed the subject.

"Where are we headed first?"

Renata stopped the golf cart in front of the hotel. She led River to a room on the lower level.

"This is a double queen room. The king size rooms look very similar, except we've placed a larger desk in them."

River entered the cooled room. They had decorated it similar to her casita, only on a smaller scale. The bathroom's finishes rivaled the luxurious ones in the casita. Each color choice and texture added to the homey feel.

"Are you busier in the fall?"

"Yes. We're often at capacity, except the week of Christmas. We have a few regulars that join us for the holiday, but it seems most people prefer a white Christmas than a mild one."

River laughed. "I agree."

Renata led her back to the golf cart and drove it along the pea gravel covered pathway to one of the larger casitas. The family casitas had to be triple the size of her little one. Similar dark wood logs and a door welcomed her onto the porch. They had painted this casita in a warm rust. The one next door was a deeper gold than her casita. The interior boasted a full kitchen with stainless steel appliances and white marble countertops. The leather furniture in the great room looked similar to the furnishings at the family's ranch house. Everything about the space screamed pricey.

"How much do these rent for?"

"We usually rent them by the week or month."

When Renata told her the price, River let out a low whistle.

"Definitely sounds like they are for high-end clientele."

"Yes, and no. Since there are six beds and two sleeper sofas, they can accommodate a family reunion. When split four ways, the price is only a few hundred more than the hotel rooms. Some families prefer the privacy of cooking in the kitchen over the dining hall. These family casitas also have a private backyard with their own hot tubs."

River followed Renata to the sliding glass doors and peered out. "Wow! That's bigger than I expected. Is that real grass?"

Renata laughed. "No. Turf that looks real. Much easier to maintain than managing both summer and winter grass."

"You have two types of grasses?"

"Many homes in the Sonoran desert—this part of Arizona—grow bermuda grass in the summer and winter rye in the cooler months. There's a few weeks where the summer grass gets scalped down to almost dirt. Then we overseed, and it takes a few more weeks before it looks good again. That entire process is too much maintenance for us. And the guests who visit before the new grass matures complain."

"Makes sense."

"Want to see the working ranch buildings?"

"Yes," River replied, barely containing her excitement.

Renata led her back to the golf cart. Then they drove back to the office and climbed into her Jeep. Renata followed a winding dirt road around a mounded hill.

River gasped. Eight buildings dotted the area—not one was visible from the resort. A large metal building with a tin roof sat at the far end.

"That's the equipment barn. We have our own small lift for hanging banners or Christmas lights on the roof. There's a small back hoe used for clearing overgrown brush and more."

As they drove past a smaller metal building, Renata told her that was the off-road vehicle garage.

"It houses the ATVs, UTVs, and a few tour Jeeps. Might be a pickup truck in there too. We have a maintenance bay and a mechanic who keeps all the equipment running."

Renata stopped in front of a long stuccoed building with a porch running the length.

"This is the men's bunkhouse. Warning, it's probably messy and smells like dirty cowboys."

River laughed as they entered. Yeah, the smell of sweat mixed with aftershave hung in the air. She held a hand near her nose to cut down the obnoxious odor.

"We can house up to twenty men in each wing if we need to. Since we've only got thirty on staff during peak season, the Vargas brothers have their own section."

"They don't live in the ranch house?"

"Only Dalton, his parents, and grandfather live in the house. His brothers moved out here years ago. They have their own single beds with end tables and a wall separating them from the rest of the bunks in the room. The center of the building is the common area. Showers, kitchen, entertainment room."

When Renata breezed through the common area and back out to her Jeep, River breathed deeper again.

"What do you say we go shopping for ranch clothes?"

"I'd love that."

After picking up River's purse from her casita, they drove into Wickenburg. Renata stopped at a western clothing store.

River's mouth dropped as they entered the vast store.

The women's section took up one third of the building. The rest was for men.

"These jeans are work jeans. Over here are fancy dress jeans. Not much selection. I think most of us buy our nice jeans elsewhere. But the men? They are particular about their dress jeans."

River remembered the pair Dalton wore the day she met him. Definitely dress jeans. Her face warmed as she recalled how they hugged his muscular thighs.

As she flipped through racks of work shirts, she grabbed six different ones. Thankfully, the store also carried wicking tank tops. Not the strappy camis she wore back home. These were u-neck in the front and came up to the base of her neck in the back. Perfect to absorb sweat under a snap front shirt. She also grabbed four pairs of work jeans, her own leather gloves, and a hat. After trying everything on, she headed to the checkout.

Once they finished in the store, they drove to a nearby café called *The Lariat*.

The quaint café looked like a cross between a French bistro and a chic western restaurant. White subway tile covered one wall behind the blond pine counter, lacquered to a glossy sheen. Black, swirly wrought-iron chairs surrounded the shiny pine tables. The art on the wall included pictures of cowboy and cowgirl couples, faces obscured by their hats. Some were kissing. Others, the hats shaded their faces. A chalkboard hung behind the counter on the tiled wall, listing all the sandwiches, salads, and specialty drinks on the menu.

A matronly woman with salt and pepper hair pulled back in a ponytail looked up from wiping down the counter. She wore a yellow frilly apron, more of the French bistro style, over a white flowy blouse and jeans. As she stepped around the counter, River noticed her bright red cowboy boots. She held her arms open wide as she walked toward them.

"Renata!"

A genuine smile spread across the woman's face as she hugged Renata.

"It's been a while."

"The resort keeps me busy."

"Who's your new friend?" the older woman asked.

"River. She's working for us part-time this summer."

"Deary, you picked a warm time of year to work here. Make sure you take care of that pale skin. Lots of sunscreen."

"Yes, ma'am," River said before Renata led her to a table.

"That's Aunt Greta. She's not our aunt. Everyone calls her that. She likes to pretend that all locals are her nieces or nephews. She never married and took over this place when her parents couldn't run it any longer. They both passed a few years ago."

"She seems nice."

"She is. I used to work here when I was in high school."

"I love the photography in here. Very artistic."

"All the pictures are of local couples. I don't know when Aunt Greta started collecting them. The couples volunteer to pose as long as their identities are concealed. Then a photographer, Cara Fullerton, takes their picture. Cara is Greta's real-life niece. Greta hangs them on the wall to sell them."

"They are so beautiful." River could picture them as cover art for her books, though her publisher would never go for it. They had their own artists and branding.

As they waited for their sandwiches, Renata asked, "So, what do you think about Dalton?"

River's cheeks warmed, and she quickly sipped her water. "He's nice."

"Just nice?"

She thought back to his story about the barbed wire. And his shirtless chest. Nice didn't adequately describe Dalton J. Vargas the fourth. He oozed masculine cowboy, even when he didn't dress the part. River's cheeks flamed at the thought.

"You like him." Renata's eyes sparkled.

River expelled a loud breath. "Yeah. I think I do like him."

"He could use someone with your sense of humor. Loosen him up."

River laughed. "He's not that bad is he?"

Renata's gaze dropped to the table. "It's taken him a long time to get over his ex. I'm just glad he broke up with her before they married."

River's heart ached for him. She knew the crushing pain of a broken engagement. Not a story she would share then.

When Aunt Greta brought their meals, Renata prayed. Then their conversation turned to Renata.

"How old are you, anyway?" River asked before she bit into her turkey and bacon club.

"Twenty-four."

"And you manage the resort alone?"

"Pretty much. When I turned eighteen, I graduated from high school early and took business classes at night. I used to have Solana's job. But a few years ago, Dalton promoted me to manager."

"Wow. And you like it?"

"I love it. I couldn't picture doing anything else. My business degree taught me what Catalina couldn't. She used to run the office before I took over."

They talked about other things, getting to know each other. By the time they finished lunch, River considered Renata a new friend. Maybe one day she would confide just how much she liked Dalton.

ON WEDNESDAY MORNING, Dalton set his travel coffee mug in the console cup holder of his truck. He placed the wrapped breakfast sandwich on the passenger seat before starting the engine. Then he ate the sandwich as he drove toward Prescott.

River Sloane had impressed him. The romance author never complained about the work. And he had worked her hard, too. Mucking stalls. Reorganizing the tack room with Dylan. Restocking everything at the resort with Renata, from the spa, dining hall, rooms, supply closets, and more. Twice he had ended up alone with her in the hot tub. Both times contrived by Renata. Both times left Dalton wanting more time with River.

He knew what his cousin was doing. She didn't hide it. Yesterday, she even suggested he take River out next weekend.

"You two are perfect for each other," Renata had said. "It's time for you to move on. I want to be an aunty."

Dalton had laughed and reminded her she would only be an aunt to Solana's kids and, at twenty-one, she was too young to get married.

Renata presented several convincing arguments. Until he reminded her that, come August first, River Sloane would head back to her home on the other side of the country.

Dalton wadded up the empty paper from his sandwich and set it on the seat. He tried to push thoughts of the blond-haired beauty from his mind. He needed to refresh his memory of what he planned to say at the Yavapai County chapter meeting. Most of the members in it ran small bed-and-breakfast places. A few owned several properties. All of them could use a modern reservation system—especially one that worked on cell phones. People Renata's age booked that way. If the business owners wanted to appeal to a younger demographic, they needed mobile-friendly systems.

He had done his research and had one in mind. His other idea had been to set up the reservation system for everyone in both chapters of the Independent Rustic Lodging Association. By offering one url, they could cross-sell other properties. He had heard about several venues doing the same in southern Arizona. They all saw an increase in business.

As he parked in front of the office in Prescott where they met, he waved to the chairwoman, Ada Wilson. She smiled and waited for him.

"I'm excited to hear about your proposal today. I think it's exactly what we need to breathe new life into our smaller business owners' properties."

"It seems to work for the southern Arizona chapter. Revenues are up fifteen percent across the board. Every property that takes part in their program is seeing growth."

"Good. That's exactly what we need."

Dalton held the door open for her and several other members. Once the meeting started, he stood at the podium and explained the plan. Smiles adorned the faces of every business owner. When Ada led the group in a vote, all the business owners voted for the plan.

As he drove home, pride welled in his chest. His plan helped Vargas Ranch as much as the next. Now he had the commitment for funds from both chapters. All he needed was a web designer.

By the time he pulled into his parking space at home, his brothers' and cousins' trucks filled the small lot. He gathered his trash and papers and headed inside. Before joining the family for dinner, he dropped his papers on the desk in his office.

When he entered the dining room, he swallowed, hoping to moisten his suddenly dry mouth. River stood next to Renata, deep in conversation. She wore a bright green floral dress that hugged her curves and flared at her waist. It stopped just below her knees, showing off her shapely legs.

Her golden hair hung loose in waves around her shoulders. Her makeup drew his attention to her full lips. It had to be criminal to look so good.

"Earth to D4," Derin waved his hand in front of Dalton's face. "Let's eat."

When River smiled at him, he rubbed a hand across the back of his neck. As he slid onto his chair directly across from her, he scolded himself. He could not afford to fall for the romance author. Yet in one week, she had gotten under his skin like no other. A prayer of hope emerged from the edges of his mind before he stifled it. By August first, River Sloane would be gone. Back to Ohio. Out of his life forever.

Except Dalton didn't want her to leave. Everything about her pulled him closer. Heart and soul.

Had he learned nothing from that conniving witch, Janessa? She only wanted his money. How did he know River wasn't exactly like her?

"We do not deviate from Your plan. Amen."

Dalton's shoulders bunched. He had missed the closing of the prayer. He had to focus. Find some way to extract River Sloane from his brain. Maybe even his heart.

As they passed food around the table, River asked many questions about the ranch. Various family members answered, telling her about their forty employees and what each of them did.

When he caught River rubbing her shoulder for a third time, he asked, "Do you need some ibuprofen?"

Her shoulders curved forward. "Oh, thank you. Probably two."

He excused himself and brought the extra bottle from his medicine cabinet. When she handed it back to him, he shook his head. "Keep it. You may want more for later."

"Mijo," Mami said, looking at him. "What are your plans for River tomorrow?"

"You should take her on a horse ride tour of the property. It's supposed to be a little cooler tomorrow," Renata said.

River laughed. "What is cooler to you?"

"One-oh-one instead of one-oh-nine like today."

"Positively brisk." River's mouth twisted in a sardonic grin.

Dalton snorted. He loved her wit. And those eyes. And—

Why was everyone staring at him? Right. Tomorrow. Tour.

He cleared his throat. "I suppose we could do that."

"I will pack you some sandwiches," Mami said. "Make sure you take breaks in the shade."

The conversation buzzed around him again. He concentrated on eating his meal.

"How was the association meeting?" Papi asked.

"Fine. They want to move forward with the website as I described it. Now I just need to find a website designer."

River's eyes locked on his. "What kind of website?"

He described his vision and watched as her face lit up.

A grin spread across her lips. "I could do that."

Dalton stared at her blankly.

"Before I was an author, I used to work for a marketing firm. I built many similar websites, designed logos, and more."

"We would pay you, of course. Are you sure?" he asked. The last thing he wanted to do was monopolize her time with a side project.

"Absolutely. Will that get me out of mucking stalls?"

He chuckled. "Maybe. You still have a lot to learn."

As dinner wound down, Drake and Derin cleared the table and loaded the dishwasher. The rest of the family gathered in the living room.

Dalton led River to his office to discuss the website in more detail. When he pulled up the site for the southern Arizona association, she stood next to him. She leaned forward, her perfume filling his nostrils as her loose hair tickled his arm. His pulse thrummed, and he resisted the temptation to pull her into his arms.

"Oh, I recognize that reservation software."

"You do?"

"Yeah, I've added it to a few websites before. Cheesy peasy."

"So you think you can do it?"

"Yeah."

"What about your novel?"

River stood straighter. The light left her features as her eyes darted to the corner of the room, instantly causing him to regret mentioning it.

"I can work on the website. It might take me a few weeks between everything else."

"That's it?"

"Yeah. The harder part is gathering all the content from each business owner. Is that something you can coordinate?"

"I'll ask Solana to do that. Can you give her pointers on what she needs to request?"

"Of course."

When Dalton angled her direction, she moved to the other side of the desk, taking the intoxicating perfume scent with her.

"How much do you normally charge?"

She gave him an amount that was almost half of what he had budgeted.

"Are you sure?"

"It's what I charge back home. Unless you need me to design some graphics?"

"How much for that?"

River gave him prices for a package. Even adding that in, they would come in well under budget. Perfect.

"Just let me or Renata know what you need."

River agreed before he walked into the great room with

her.

Renata hadn't waited for her, so Dalton offered to drive her back to her casita over a mile away from the ranch house. Once in the truck, he thanked her again.

"I'm happy to build the website for you. This place is so amazing."

You're amazing, he thought.

As hard as it was, he stayed in the truck instead of walking her to her door. It wasn't a date. He had no legitimate reason to escort her, despite how much he wanted to. At least he would have her undivided attention tomorrow on their horse ride.

7

RIVER SHOT UPRIGHT in the dark room, sweat drenching her hairline and neck. Disoriented, she looked around the unfamiliar room. She flopped back on the pillows, her head sinking deep into them, as she remembered the casita. Arizona. Dalton.

Sighing, she threw back the covers and walked to the kitchenette. The dim blue light on the microwave read twelve sixteen. She found a bottle of chilled water in the apartment-sized fridge. Unscrewing the top, she tilted her head back and gulped the cool liquid, listening for any sound that might have woken her.

Nothing.

River wandered over to the desk in front of the dark window, flipping on the small desk light. She punched the power button on her laptop and eased into the cushy leather office chair. After tucking her wireless earbuds in place, she tapped on her phone a few times until loud, high energy music reverberated in her head. She opened the special software she used for writing and created a new project.

Dalton's story from the hot tub had rolled around in her mind for a week. River drummed her fingers on the desk as she pondered her yet-to-be-written cowboy romance.

Stubborn single rancher?

No. Too hard to write a series starting like that.

Five brothers, like the Vargases?

No. Too obvious. She didn't want her books to become easily connected with the family. She knew the price of fame. On the one hand, it could increase their visitors. On the other… Too risky.

Three brothers?

Yes. Three brothers would be a good start. Potential for a short series if her publisher liked the idea. Enough to test the waters as a cowboy romance author.

She grabbed her electronic notebook and scratched down three male character names and three female character names. Normally, she wrote detailed character sketches with personalities, family relationships, and major events from their pasts. This time, she skipped it all and started writing.

Words flowed. Ideas formed. The personality of her hero took shape. Similar to Dalton, but not the same. Her heroine fled to Arizona to escape an abusive ex-boyfriend. Her heart needed time to heal. She needed a job.

Write what you know.

A designer. Someone who could work remotely. Just like River would build a website for Dalton, her heroine would do the same for the handsome oldest brother. No, she would start with the middle brother.

Words traveled from her creative soul through her fingertips into the laptop. Chapter after chapter. A quick sip of warm water. More words. Scenes. Settings. Sights. Smells.

Her phone chimed, and she jerked as her heart raced. She paused her music and read the message.

Dalton. *Missed you at breakfast. Still up for the ride?*

River yanked the earbuds out, stowing them in their case. Then she glanced up at the window. Early morning light blazed across the sky.

What time was it, anyway?

Seven.

River stood slowly and looked at her novel. Five chapters. Nearly ten thousand words in seven hours. She snorted. Seven hours she should have used to sleep. Rubbing a hand over her face, she considered her options.

She texted Dalton back. Need forty minutes. Pick me up?

Then she spent ten of it re-reading the first chapter. Tweaked a few words. Copied it into a protected document and sent it off to her publisher. After she powered off her laptop, she hurried through a shower. She left her hair wet and braided it. One thing she had learned about Arizona, it would dry quickly and she might appreciate the coolness on her back during the horse ride until it dried.

River had just finished sliding her feet into the comfy brown boots when a knock sounded on the door. She grabbed her hat and hurried to answer it.

Goodness. Could Dalton look any better with his tan face, eyes shining with his smile?

"Morning sleepyhead."

"Ah—"

Her phone pinged, and she glanced at it. Her publisher.

"I need a second."

Excellent start. Can't wait to read more.

River sucked in a deep breath. Her shoulders rose and fell as she blew it out.

"Everything okay?"

Heat warmed her cheeks.

"I didn't exactly sleep last night."

Dalton quirked a well-groomed eyebrow. Maybe it was her lack of sleep. He seemed twice as charming this morning.

"I wrote five chapters. That's why I missed breakfast. And sleep."

When his shoulders dropped, she rushed to explain. "I'm still up for our ride and picnic. I'm kinda wired, actually. My publisher loved the first chapter."

"Are you sure?"

"Yeah. Can we stop for a—"

Dalton thrust an iced mocha in her hand and he held up a paper-wrapped breakfast sandwich in the other.

She shoved her hat on her head and accepted both.

"Drake said you hadn't been by, so I asked him what your favorite drink was. Hopefully, mocha is right."

River giggled. Oh, boy. The lack of sleep might be getting to her more than she thought.

"It is."

Dalton held his truck door open for her before he rounded to the other side. River scarfed down the breakfast sandwich after a few sips of the sweet coffee drink. By the time they arrived at the stables, she finished both the sandwich and coffee. Feeling re-energized, she held high hopes for the day.

"Unlike your hippie grandparents, I will not spoil you. Well, I guess I did with breakfast. Anyway, today you'll groom and saddle your own horse."

"As long as you teach me what I need to know, I don't mind."

Dalton's grin lit his entire face. Then he guided her past several stalls before stopping at a gentle palomino mare.

"This is Sunflower."

River snorted. "You can't be serious. You're having me ride a horse that shares a name with my mother?"

"I thought it was funny." Lines formed by his eyes, and one corner of his mouth twitched.

"I might have to call her Flower."

Dalton shrugged, playfulness softening his features, and making those gold eyes sparkle. She could stare into them all day long.

River cleared her throat. "Fine. Sunflower is just fine."

He placed a bridle on Sunflower's head and clipped a lead to it. He showed River how to hold the rope and lead the horse to the grooming area. Then he secured the horse and retrieved his own, a beautiful bay gelding.

"This is Toasted Toffee."

River snickered.

"Yeah, the moral of that story is: don't let Drake name

your horse. It will end up with some sort of coffee or special-ty drink name."

"I love it."

Once his horse was secured, Dalton ran down a list of safe ways to work with the horses. He described the steps and tools. They started by picking the horses's hooves. He showed her on his horse and helped her start on hers. She felt tiny and a little fragile as she rested the animal's large hoof above her knee. When Dalton's arms circled her, she relaxed. He placed one hand over hers as she held the hoof pick. Then he gently guided her hand, digging the dirt from Sunflower's hoof.

"That doesn't hurt her, does it?"

"No. Relax," he whispered in her ear.

Yeah, like she could relax with his nearness, sending waves of warmth radiating through her body. If she turned her head to her right, would his lips be close enough to kiss?

"They can sense your feelings and will react to them."

River released a calming breath. Dalton eased away from her and focused on his horse.

"Remember, easy movements. Always let the horse know where you are. If you're not sure what to do, stay put and ask."

"Got it, boss."

The remaining steps using different brushes and combs made River less nervous. She found the movements relax-ing. When Sunflower let out what sounded like a sigh, she smiled.

"She likes you," Dalton said.

"I like her, too."

When it came time to saddle her mare, Dalton walked her through the process. Goodness, the saddle was heavier than she expected. She supposed if she saddled a horse more often, she would build up strength.

Once both horses were saddled, they led them outside. Dalton gave her a leg up before he mounted his horse, his movements fluid and easy. Then they rode out to the field, as he called it.

The further away from the resort they rode, River felt almost as if she had been transported back to a simpler time. Bright blue sky stretched overhead from horizon to horizon. The sun warmed her back as much as the man riding next to her warmed her heart. Scrub brush and the occasional tree dotted the tall grass. It was just her, Dalton, their horses, and the wide open wilderness. She could almost picture a life here.

DALTON DONNED HIS aviator sunglasses, allowing him to study River closely without coming across as creepy. She smiled and propped one hand on the top of her new hat as she tilted her head to face the sun. A content hum rose from her throat. In moments like this, next to her on his family's ranch, he could almost forget she didn't belong here.

An ache started somewhere around his heart. He wished she could belong here. Like this. Riding with him. Waiting for him back at the ranch house at the end of his day, giddy from writing her romance novels. Hazel eyes eager to see him.

"So, where do you keep the cattle? I think I read online that this is a working cattle ranch, right?"

It was foolish to dream, despite what Mami said. River came from another world, blatantly obvious from her question. She was a city girl from the other side of the nation.

"We own thirty-five thousand acres. The cattle rotate from pasture to pasture. Right now, they're on the north side of Dalton Peak."

"Will we see them today?"

"From a distance, yes."

He wouldn't take her too close. Not until she learned

more about the cattle. Who was he kidding? She wouldn't be here long enough to learn. He had to get that fact through his thick skull.

Dalton scanned the horizon. Puffy white clouds speckled the sky far from them. Possibly a sign of a monsoon storm later. The forecast hadn't called for rain that day. Still, he knew a monsoon storm could flare up in the right conditions, catching even the weather people off guard.

As they rode toward Verde Wash, Dalton slowed Toffee. The mesquite and palo verde trees would provide shade while they stopped to rest the horses and enjoy their lunch.

A loud, high-pitched buzzing came from overhead. His head snapped up as he found the source.

"What's that?" River asked.

"Drone."

Mami probably asked a cowboy to fly it for her so she could spy on him. Although, it sounded different from their model.

After he dismounted, he tied Toffee to a tree before helping River down from her horse. She moaned as soon as her feet touched the ground.

"Ah, yeah. Little sore." She offered him a wan smile.

"Walk around a bit while I find a spot for lunch."

River shuffled away.

He took Sunflower's reins and tied her near Toffee. Then he unpacked the soft cooler from his saddlebags, along with a blanket.

Those white clouds in the distance bothered him. They had moved closer and grew in size, billowing high into the sky. Too far away to send water into Verde Wash. Still, he would face that direction while they ate.

The drone followed him fifty feet overhead, making him uneasy. He dropped the cooler and blanket by a palo verde tree on the bank of the wash. Then he went back to his saddlebags for his binoculars. Sure enough, that drone wasn't Vargas owned.

Could be someone from the Bureau of Land Management checking on their nearby land. Though, the BLM surveyors knew the Vargas property lines. It was unlikely they would fly over the ranch.

"River!" He motioned her to join him under the shade of the palo verde tree, hoping it would hide them from the drone.

He offered her a chilled bottle of water, loosening the cap for her. She took a few sips.

"Is it one of yours?" she asked as she sat on the blanket next to him.

"No." The tension corded his shoulders.

"Should we worry?"

Dalton ignored her question and handed her a sandwich. He wasn't sure, and he didn't want to frighten her.

"It couldn't be…"

When her voice faded, his eyes locked with hers. She looked away as creases formed on her forehead. Odd.

"River? Talk to me."

"There's this guy. It couldn't be him. There's no way he could know where I am."

The hair on Dalton's neck stood on end. He straightened his back.

"What guy? What do you mean?"

"Back in Ohio, I had a stalker. Not a *stalker* stalker. But a man overly interested in where I went. I ran into him at the grocery store. The bank. The coffee shop when I met with friends."

He frowned. "Isn't that the definition of a stalker?"

"Maybe. No. I don't think so. He never acted like fans do. Never asked for an autograph or anything like that. It just seemed weird that we ended up in the same places at the same time. Columbus isn't a small town. Statistically, it would have been nearly impossible to cross paths so many times without it being deliberate. It wasn't on my part, but I could never figure out if it was on his."

Shooting down a drone came with a hefty fine, especially if it was a BLM drone. Dalton considered it. What if it was her stalker? He would feel responsible if something happened to River and he could have stopped it.

"Who knows that you are staying here?"

"My publisher. Her assistant. My parents. That's it. I didn't even tell my friends. I just said I had to travel for work. Not where."

He didn't think his employees would have told anyone. They had had other famous people stay at the resort and never had an incident. He made it clear to all employees, he would fire them if they leaked private information about any guest, famous or not.

"It's probably not him. I mean, how would he even know I'm here?"

When she finally angled toward him, he held her gaze for several seconds. She bit her lower lip, doing little to erase his concern.

Suddenly, she smiled. "Don't worry about it. It's impossible. We should enjoy lunch."

Dalton resolved to keep a close watch on both the weather and the drone. For the time being, its buzzing sounded further away.

He propped himself on one hand. River reached over and squeezed it.

"Hey, I'm sure it's nothing. Probably just some hikers, right?"

He held back a frown and ate a big bite of his sandwich. It definitely wasn't hikers. Most folks didn't hike in the heat of summer during lunch time. Early morning, maybe. Not at noon.

"So what are these trees called, with the green trunks?"

A smile twitched at the corner of his mouth. "Palo verde. Verde meaning green. Palo meaning stick."

"The yellow flowers are pretty."

He snorted. "They are pretty—annoying, that is. These

are the Desert Museum variety. They bloom in the summer. It's what we've planted around the resort too, so the worst of the litter from the flowers is during the off-peak season. They get everywhere."

"Good to know." She ate a few bites of her sandwich while he answered.

"When the monsoon storms blow through, most of the blooms will clear out."

"And the big cactuses with arms?"

Dalton laughed. "Saguaro. And the plural of cactus is cacti, Miss Romance Writer."

"Right. That's what editors are for."

When she winked at him, he smiled. He loved her joking.

A gust of wind whipped at the branches overhead, dropping the yellow blooms on them. His eyes darted to the sky. The clouds had moved closer and brewed into the beginnings of a storm. Much closer now, dark gray covering their underbelly.

"We need to pack up and head back. I don't like the look of those clouds."

River jerked and let out a squeal. "Was that lightning?"

Not good.

He shot to his feet and gathered up the blanket and the rest of their uneaten lunch. After he stowed everything in his saddlebags, he gave her a leg up, then mounted Toffee. The wind whipped forcefully against them. River's hat blew off her head. The string kept it from blowing away completely.

When a wall of dust rolled closer, his mind raced. They had to get out of there.

"Put your shirt up over your nose and mouth!" he yelled at her.

River's eyes widened, but she did what he asked. He yanked a bandanna from his pocket and tied it over his nose and mouth, wishing he had thought to bring her one.

"Can you ride fast?"

When she hesitated, he motioned her forward. They needed shelter, and fast. The wash wasn't it. Too dangerous.

As they trotted toward Dalton Peak, it blocked the worst of the wind. Then he spotted it. The old drover's cabin. It wasn't much, but it would protect them from the lightning and the rain. He hoped.

He glanced over his shoulder and pointed toward the dilapidated wooden structure. When she nodded, he kicked Toffee to a canter. Another glance told him she followed close behind, matching his pace. Toffee danced to the side when the wall of dust hit them hard. He slowed his horse. River rode beside him, squinting as the dust pelted her face.

Then he smelled it through the bandanna. They wouldn't make it to the cabin in time. Still, he pressed on.

8

THE SWEET FRAGRANCE of the creosote bush carried on the wind, blasting Dalton's face. It signaled that the skies were about to break under the weight of rain. A few more yards.

The sky darkened overhead to a deep blue-gray. A loud yell caught his attention. He pulled up and wheeled Toffee around. River's horse had no rider!

A lump constricted his throat. He rode over to Sunflower and grabbed her reins as his eyes frantically darted over the landscape. His heart assaulted his chest like a jackhammer against concrete.

Splat. Plop. Splat. Plop. Rain gushed from the sky as lightning flashed from cloud to ground.

Where was she? *Lord, please.*

A hand shot in the air, and he rode toward it. He was at her side, holding both sets of reins, not aware of having dismounted.

"River!"

The loud rain drowned out her response. Water soaked both of them, coming down in sheets. Angry, muddy water gushed through the wash a few feet behind her, creeping ever closer. He had to get her out of there.

He kneeled beside her, yanking his bandanna down. "Can you walk or ride?"

She shook her head and shouted over the violent downpour, "My ankle!"

Then she touched her right leg.

Dalton transferred the reins to his other hand. Then he wrapped his arm around River's waist and hauled her to her feet. Lightning flashed like a choreographed concert right before thunder shook the ground so hard it tickled his chest. The water in the wash lapped dangerously close.

They had to go now.

"Climb on my back! Arms around my neck!" he commanded as he crouched to make it easier.

Thunder clapped its deafening warning. Flashes of light danced across the sky.

River balanced on one foot and launched against his back. His arm wrapped around her good leg. He reached for the other while keeping tight hold of the horses. If it came to it, he would drop the reins and let the animals fend for themselves. She was more important.

Though River wasn't heavy, the rain made her jeans slippery against his shirt sleeves. She clasped her wrists together, angled across his neck and chest, careful not to choke him. He summoned every ounce of his strength and dug each foot into the ground, propelling them ever closer to the drover's cabin. One foot in front of the other. Rain blurred his vision when his hat whipped off, lodging between his head and River.

As another bolt of lightning lit up the sky, Toffee pranced and Sunflower reared up, straining against his hold. He let the leathers slip from his hand and readjusted his hold on River.

Please, Lord, let the horses make it back to the ranch. Help me get River to safety.

Just one more yard and they would be there.

Dalton let out a guttural howl as he gave it his all. He dipped his shoulder and ran full force. The door flung wide, its hinges squawking loudly. He lost his footing and tumbled to the floor, taking the brunt of the impact. With his booted foot, he kicked the door closed.

Then his arms went limp. His chest burned from the physical toll. River slid off his back, breathing just as hard as he was.

The rain beating on the tin roof sounded like a roaring crowd at a Cardinal's football game. A smile turned up one side of his mouth. How nice of them to cheer for him.

"Dalton?" River's voice shook.

He rolled onto his side and pushed up with his elbow. "You okay?"

She nodded as she removed her hat from around her neck. He found his resting on the floor. When he studied her, he noticed red rimming her eyes.

Dalton placed his hand on her cheek. "Does it hurt?"

"I... I'm sorry."

Her shoulders shook. He gathered her onto his lap and into his arms as he leaned back against the wall.

"Shh."

He rocked her back and forth until the sobs subsided, stroking her water-logged braid.

A chill ran down his spine. The temperature dropped a good twenty degrees. Maybe more. Not cold, but it felt like it after the sweltering heat from an hour ago.

"I'm sorry," River whispered.

Dalton held her away from him. "What are you sorry for?"

"Falling off Sunflower."

"Given the circumstances, I'm surprised you stayed on as long as you did."

She screwed up her face and playfully swatted at his arm.

Then it hit him. How good it felt to hold her. To share space with her. To touch her cheek. Her back. The electricity in the air had nothing to do with the storm raging outside the walls of the drover's cabin. River's features relaxed and her eyes roamed over his face. His gaze dropped to her lips.

Full. Inviting.

His eyes shot back to hers. He swore she nodded her head slightly. Had she?

Then she leaned closer. His arms tightened around her back as his lips brushed across hers. His heart raced as he deepened the kiss, longing for her touch and her heart. She ran her fingers through his dripping wet hair. He lodged his hand into her tangled braid. Fire burned inside of him, but he contained it as he savored the softness of her lips melding with his. This woman. How could he feel so fiercely for her, having only met her a week ago? She turned his world and his heart upside down.

He slowed the kiss. Then teased her by brushing his lips softly across hers. Once. Twice more.

At last, he gently nudged her away from him. Just a few inches. Enough that he could look into her eyes again.

River released a soft breath as a smile stretched across those maddening, swollen lips. Then she slid off his lap onto the floor. Her eyes sparkled, and he knew she was about to toss a zinger his way.

"You look like a drowned rat, Dalton."

He rubbed his hands on his thighs as he chuckled from the depths of his soul.

"You look perfect," he said, grinning.

She rewarded him with one of her own.

Before he thought about kissing her again, he pushed up off the floor and took stock of the cabin. The place was filthy. Thick cobwebs and dust coated every surface. He suspected it hadn't been used actively in his lifetime.

The room they had landed in held no furniture. Only an old iron stove from the turn of the century. A few hooks lined the wall. Dalton set both of their hats on the hooks. Then he jiggled the handle on the door to another room. Locked. He could probably bust it open, but it didn't seem worth the energy. The room they were in provided the shelter they needed.

"What now?" River asked.

The rain continued to beat steadily against the tin roof. Peals of thunder sounded in the distance.

"We wait it out. How's that ankle?"

"It hurts. I don't think I can put weight on it."

Dalton found an old, rusted bucket in the corner. He turned it on its side and gently lifted her leg. Slowly, he rested her foot on top of the bucket. He carefully removed her boot and sock, despite her sharp intake of air. Swollen. Already.

He ran a hand through his hair. Then he patted each of his pockets. Pocket knife. Gum. A soggy receipt for something no longer legible. His cell phone. He pulled it from his drenched shirt pocket. A stream of water trailed down his arm from the device, the screen black.

"How's your phone look?"

River cringed. She shifted onto her hip and retrieved it from her back pocket. Cracks covered the dark screen.

"I landed on that side."

When she dropped her hands on her legs, drops of water sprayed the floor. They were both soaked to the bone. He wasn't sure if wringing out their clothes would be useful or not. He had worn a t-shirt under his snap front shirt. Wondered if she did, too.

He turned his back and removed the snap front shirt. Then squeezed as much water out of it as he could before he draped it over a hook on the wall.

One thing was certain. They weren't going anywhere for a while.

RIVER SAVORED THE memory of Dalton's comforting arms and wonderful kisses. The feelings between them had been building since his barbed wire story. She shouldn't fall for him. Couldn't fall for him. Yet, she was. Those kisses stirred a yearning in her that no one else ever had. She wanted to be close to Dalton — to fall in love despite all the logical reasons it made no sense.

The throbbing in her ankle became too much to ignore. River forced her panic down. The storm had stranded them in the drover's cabin. No communication. No horses. Her swollen ankle was certain to buckle under her weight. How were they going to get back to the resort? Surely, his family would come for them, wouldn't they?

When Dalton wrung out his outer shirt, she mirrored his actions. Her tank top underneath was just as drenched. Even her bra felt waterlogged. She wouldn't take either of those off. Not with her rugged cowboy a few feet away.

"What happens when we don't come back?" she asked, trying to keep the fear from her tone. She needed to know how long they would be stranded.

Dalton's eyes darted away. Not the reaction she had hoped for. Nor did it calm her fear.

"If the horses make it back without us, then my brothers will organize a search party. When the weather clears. They'll have the UTVs, which will make it go faster."

"And if the horses don't make it back?"

"It might take them longer to realize they need to search for us."

"Dalton, how long?"

He leaned a shoulder against the cabin wall and crossed one booted foot over the other.

"When we don't show for dinner, they'll text. Knowing Mami, she'll text a dozen times and raise the alarm. They knew our plans and they know me. They'll start as soon as they think something is wrong."

"But?" She heard the word in his tone even though he hadn't said it.

"But they might not find us until tomorrow."

"Tomorrow!"

River's chest heaved as panic clawed the back of her throat.

"Calm down. We're safe here. It's not leaking. Or flooding."

Could she handle a night alone in the wilderness? Couldn't coyotes attack them?

"The door closes. It'll keep coyotes out."

Had she voiced her fears aloud? Ugh.

She wasn't sure the door closing was such a good thing. It would keep her confined with the cowboy she was falling for. What could go wrong?

The exhaustion from her lack of sleep last night, combined with the stress of the situation, made her want to curl up and nap.

"River." His deep voice brought a flicker of calm to her spiraling thoughts.

Her eyes locked on Dalton's gold ones. She swallowed the lump in her throat.

"You're safe. I won't let anything happen to you."

Her gaze traveled from his damp mussed hair down his clingy white t-shirt, all the way to his feet. He was strong. He had carried her on his back through sheets of rain to this dilapidated old cabin. Nothing would get past the solid man.

The last of her energy faded. She closed her eyes and rested her head against the wall. She would have to trust God to watch over her. And Dalton J. Vargas the fourth.

9

_____

RIVER'S HEAD DROPPED to the side, jolting her from a nap. The sweet smell of the rain seemed stronger. She opened her eyes, blinking away the remnants of sleep. Dalton stood in the doorway of the drover's cabin, shoulder resting against the frame, staring at the horizon. He looked relaxed. Something about him made her want to stand behind him and wrap her arms around his waist. Rest her head against his back. Hold him close for hours. She felt completely safe with him.

Shaking off the delectable thoughts, she asked, "Still raining?"

He continued staring out the door. "Misting."

She stretched, knocking her foot off the bucket. Waves of pain ricocheted through her and she whimpered. Dalton rushed to her side.

"Let me help you."

"I need to move around. How long was I out?"

His concerned gold eyes softened. "An hour."

She placed her hands on his calloused ones. Then he yanked her to her feet before he looped his arm around her waist.

"Still hurting?"

River sucked in a sharp breath and nodded.

"What time is it?"

He flicked his wrist to look at his watch. "Four."

She let out a slow breath as he helped her rest against the wall. He stepped back and leaned against the opposite wall. The silence settled over them again. So, she made up things to talk about.

"Besides tamales, what's your favorite food?"

Dalton chuckled. "Smoked brisket. Padre used to smoke meat once a week. Before his hip replacement. Now it pains him when he stands too long. Been meaning to ask him how to make it myself."

"He would probably enjoy sitting in a chair on the porch telling you what to do."

He snorted. "Yeah. He and Papi like to tell me what to do."

Hearing the frustration in his voice, she decided not to unpack that.

Instead, she asked, "So you like to cook?"

"I grill sometimes. Figure using a smoker wouldn't be too difficult to learn."

River rubbed a hand on her arm, nervous.

"What about you? What's your favorite food?" he asked.

"Beef lo mein. I could eat Chinese food nearly every day of the week."

Dalton laughed. "It's been forever since I've had Chinese. I wonder if our chef could put it on the menu."

"You're the boss man. I'm sure you can make that happen. Favorite color?"

"Blue."

"Green. Favorite animal?" She held up her hand. "Wait! Let me guess. Horse?"

He chuckled. "Dog. I've always wanted a dog."

"Really? Why don't you have one? Couldn't you get a cattle dog?"

"Drake's allergic to dogs and cats. Triggers his asthma, so we never had a pet dog."

"Doesn't he still live in the bunkhouse?"

"Yeah. I'm the only brother that lives in the ranch house

with Papi, Mami, and Padre."

"Then why couldn't you get a dog now?"

He rubbed a hand over his five o'clock shadow. "I suppose I could."

"What kind of dog would you get?"

"Dunno. Probably one from a shelter. How about you?"

"I love dogs, too. Always wanted one, but never liked the idea of keeping one in my cramped apartment."

When his smile faded, she wished she hadn't mentioned home. Oddly, she hadn't been the least bit homesick. Not even stranded with him in the musty old shack.

Dalton dropped his arms, and they hung loosely at his sides. His eyes darted to the corner of the room.

"Can I ask a really personal question?" he asked.

"Sure."

"Have you ever been married?"

That old pain pierced her heart for a few seconds. "Nope."

"Close?"

River glanced away as the memories brought the familiar regret. "I thought I loved a man once. We weren't on the same page. It didn't work out."

"I know what that's like."

Janessa. Yeah, she remembered what his brothers said about the woman.

"How old are you?"

River rested a hand on her chest, and fake frowned, feigning offense. "Don't you know you're not supposed to ask a woman her age?"

Dalton shrugged as his eyes glimmered. A smile twitched in the corner of his mouth.

She flashed a half-smile. "I'll be thirty-one on Tuesday."

His eyes rounded and he pointed his finger toward the ground rapidly as he straightened. He pushed away from the wall. "This Tuesday? The fourth of July?"

"Yup. I share a birthday with our nation."

"Wow. I don't think I've ever met anyone born on a holiday before."

River snorted. "I used to think the fireworks were for me. Silly kid."

"My birthday is April eighteenth."

"And?"

"Age? Thirty-four."

"Wow. You old geezer you." She winked to soften her sarcasm. "How old are your brothers?"

"Dylan is your age. Thirty-one. Derin is twenty-eight, going on sixteen."

River snorted. "I sense you two don't exactly get along."

"We don't. He's always flirting with the guests. When God handed out confidence, he received a double portion. Unfortunately, it makes him think he's God's gift to the world."

"At least you have siblings."

"Some days, I don't think you're missing anything. Anyway, Devon is twenty-four and Drake is twenty-one."

"Oh, I thought they were older than that. That means you're thirteen years older than the youngest."

He leaned against the wall again. "I see you are good at math."

River laughed. "Math, sarcasm, and writing. My three superpowers."

Dalton smiled before suddenly turning serious. "Why did you come here? I mean, you've surprised me by mucking the stalls like a champ and all the physical labor. I'll give you that. But it seems like there is more to the story."

River slid down the wall to sit on the ground again. Dalton took a few steps toward her before sitting in front of her cross-legged. Close enough for a quiet conversation, but far enough not to touch.

After expelling a deep breath, she answered.

"My first book was published six years ago. I used to work at a marketing firm during the day. Then I came home and wrote. My first three novels weren't great. I've never shown them to anyone. When I finished my fourth, I submitted it to my current publisher. At first, they weren't looking for workplace tropes. They sent me a letter rejecting it, but they suggested I work through their manuscript readiness courses online."

"So, no but not no?"

"Yeah. I was disappointed, but had too much time on my hands in the evenings. My ex had broken up with me. It was watch TV while eating ice cream, or take their courses."

"Let me guess. You took the courses."

"Yup. Then I reworked my manuscript. Strengthened some of the secondary tropes and resubmitted it. They loved the new version and signed me for a three-book deal. After the second book, I earned enough to go part-time with my marketing job."

Dalton's undivided attention surprised her. He seemed genuinely interested, so she continued.

"That first three-book series shot to the top of the best-seller lists. I couldn't believe it. Over the past six years, they've published ten of my books. The best part? They're Christian and I can include Christian themes."

"So it's not all attraction and lust?"

River snorted. "Attraction that turns to love. No lust. I write wholesome stories. Lots of women prefer them too."

His intense gaze sent shivers down her spine.

"It's ironic that I write about falling in love, yet am so terrible at it myself. I've only had two boyfriends ever. One was the typical only-during-high-school-break-up-before-college. The other... He dumped me faster than a formula one race car when I found Jesus."

Dalton frowned and straightened his spine. River held up one hand.

"I know. I'm better off without him. It took me a few years to get over him. But I had Jesus and church friends to help me through it."

A shadow fell over his face and his eyes darted away. River stilled her fidgety hands and watched Dalton. Furrowed brow. Hurt eyes. She wanted to touch him. Hold him. Help him.

"Janessa." His voice creaked, and he cleared his throat. "She had been a guest."

Ah. It made sense. This hard working man's entire world revolved around the ranch and resort. She figured it had to be hard to meet or make time for someone unless she stepped into his world.

Like her.

She ignored the thought, not ready to admit anything. He continued.

"The short version of the story is that I fell prey to her flirting. She made me feel special. Like I was more than just a rancher. I asked her to stay, and she did. Foolish me for never questioning how she could leave a job with no notice."

He cleared his throat.

"She worked in the office with Renata. Solana was still in high school back then. Once Janessa found out how much money the ranch makes, she manipulated me into a proposal."

When his eyes glistened and he looked away, River's heart melted faster than an ice cube on a sunny Arizona day.

"I caught her… At least I found out before I married her and she stole half the ranch."

His brothers hadn't been kidding. The woman sounded positively evil. Cruella De Vil had nothing on her.

"I feel like such an idiot. Falling in love with a two-faced, scheming woman."

When his shoulders sagged, she scooted closer and reached for his hands.

"I might not be an expert on true love, but I've observed plenty of relationships over the years. We can't always choose who we fall in love with or when. Common sense and internal pep talks make little difference. When love inconveniently turns our lives upside down, we're left with a series of choices. We have to decide what will we give up to pursue that love and what we won't."

She released his hands, her own words churning a new thread of thoughts in her soul. What would she give up for the sake of love?

"I decided not to give up my relationship with Jesus. It has always been more important to me than any earthly love. I just hope He'll let me find someone while I'm still young enough to have kids."

Dalton's eyes searched hers, and the full impact of her words slammed against her chest. She was falling in love with this sweet cowboy. Soft and sensitive on the inside. Loves dogs. Puts his dreams, however small they may be, on hold for the good of his family. Him. Dalton J. Vargas the fourth was who her heart wanted.

DALTON COULDN'T EXPLAIN what came over him. All his secret dreams and hurts gushed from his mouth. Letting River in was dangerous. She wouldn't stay. She would leave him. Go back to her home thousands of miles away. He would be crushed. Heartbroken again.

She had one thing right. No internal pep talk could convince his heart to stop drawing closer to her. He saw the train wreck coming and was completely powerless to stop it.

He cleared his throat and reiterated his earlier question.

"Why are you here?"

"Oh, yeah. I never did answer that. My last two books are underperforming and I'm under contract for three more. Cowboy romances are crazy hot right now and my publisher gave me the choice between cowboy or Amish."

Dalton's head jerked back, and he chuckled. "Amish? I definitely can't picture you writing something like that."

The way she scrunched up her face had him laughing inside.

"Me either. I didn't think I could write cowboy romance. I know nothing about your lifestyle. Or at least I didn't."

His heart thrummed in his chest. "But you think you can. What changed your mind?"

"You."

Air stuck in his chest. His pulse raced, and his heart yearned to be important to her—despite all the sirens in his head warning him away from a relationship with her.

"Watching you. You've inspired me. I guess you could say you are my muse."

Was that good? Did that mean she was interested in him? She had let him kiss her. She even returned his kiss, stirring a longing in him stronger than he had ever felt.

"I think I said too much." She glanced at the floor.

No. Don't stop.

River pulled her braid over her shoulder and loosened it. While she looked at the corner of the room, she finger-combed it. Did she have any idea how incredibly sexy she looked right now?

"Tell me about it," he whispered, wanting to keep her talking, prolonging the connection with her.

"My book?" She snorted. "You don't want to hear about a romance book."

"I do." To his surprise, he really did. It was important to her, so he wanted to know about it.

"I'm breaking all the rules. My entire process—I've tossed it aside with this one. Last night... Goodness, was that really last night? I remembered your barbed wire story. My mind started churning."

She glanced away. "Honestly, I fell asleep right away, but then I woke up at midnight."

River let out a slow breath, her shoulders rising and falling with the effort.

"The words were just there. It's hard to explain. Some

books are like that. The idea smacks me upside my head. The words flow. It's almost like the Spirit breathed into me and I can't stop writing. Those are my favorite books. It becomes about something bigger than just River Sloane. There's a message."

"What's the message in this book?" he asked, eager to know more.

"Everything in life is about God's timing, His design. Even when we don't see it. Even when circumstances make little sense. Like me coming to Vargas Ranch. When I boarded that plane last week, I did not know…"

Her words faded. He watched awe march across her face before shyness replaced it.

"If someone would have told me, I would be eager to get back to a casita to write a cowboy romance after being stranded with a good-looking one for hours—"

He couldn't resist. "You think I'm good-looking?"

River rolled her eyes and scoffed. "Duh, Dalton. I let you kiss me."

"Want me to kiss you again? You know, just to be sure."

When she scrunched up her face again, Dalton laughed. He really liked when she did that.

"Maybe later, cowboy."

He roared. "Is that a promise?"

River shrugged. "Where was I? Oh yeah, my book."

She cleared her throat.

"I usually map out the characters. Their personalities, strengths, weaknesses, backstory. The conflicts I plan to weave into the story. This time? None of that. I just started writing about this working guest ranch in Arizona. Three brothers who lost their parents in a tragic commuter plane crash when the oldest had just turned eighteen."

"Wow. That's harsh."

"Well, they need some baggage in their past to make it an interesting story."

He nodded. Made sense.

"Anyway, I'm starting with the middle brother. He's the outgoing one."

"Like Derin."

"Eh. Maybe like a cross between Devon and…"

"And?"

"You. Please don't be mad."

Dalton smiled as warmth settled in his chest. "I'm honored that you think I'm interesting enough for a romance story. I'm pretty boring. Hard working. Devoted to this place."

"Yeah, that's the appeal."

When River snapped her lips tightly together, he sensed she hadn't meant to say that.

"Anyway, the heroine is fleeing an abusive ex with her nine-month-old son."

"Sounds complicated and intense."

"Yup. Someone like me would make a terrible character. Not enough drama. My fictional heroine is much more interesting. The makings of a bestseller. I hope. I try not to think about that while I'm writing. Just write the story as the characters dictate."

He craned his head to the side. "The characters tell you what to write?"

"Usually. I know it sounds weird. It's just how it feels to me. I get to know them, almost like friends. Then I listen and put their words on the page. I pray about the stories too. What does God want me to write?"

"It sounds amazing, River. You are really talented."

She snorted. "You have read none of it. It could be horrid."

"I wouldn't believe it. You are an amazing woman. Big heart. Smart."

Beautiful. His sweet River.

Dalton swallowed hard. His heart was gone, gone, gone. And he wasn't too certain he wanted to do anything about it.

The hum of a motor drew his attention. He pulled himself from his thoughts and sprang to his feet, looking out the door. The rain had stopped. In the distance, he saw the silver UTV headed their way.

"They found us," he said. "Stay put. Let me flag them down."

Without waiting for her response, he jogged toward the vehicle. He hollered while he waved his arms in the air. A flick of the lights acknowledged they had spotted him.

Derin revved the UTV faster over the uneven terrain. Devon held the grab bar on the passenger's side. The vehicle skidded to a stop next to him.

"River with you?" Derin asked.

"Yeah. Sprained or broken ankle."

Derin's face shadowed. It felt strange to see his normally jovial brother so concerned.

"Let me get her," Dalton said as his brothers exited the vehicle.

Devon jogged around the UTV and entered the shack behind him. River tried to scooch up the wall on her own.

"Hang on. Let me help," Dalton said, hurrying to her side.

"Let's see that ankle," Devon said as he flicked his phone's flashlight on.

Dalton's stomach clenched. Deep purple bruises covered her swollen ankle. When she tried to place any weight on it, she whimpered.

10

RIVER STARTLED WHEN Dalton bolted to his feet. Heat flamed her face. She couldn't believe she had revealed so much about her book or her feelings. Dalton had a way about him that compelled her to share her heart and soul with him. Even though she liked him, it scared her. She had let no one near that sacred place of her heart—the place where stories were born.

He quickly returned with his brother Devon in tow. Devon shined his flashlight on her messed up ankle. Her stomach tightened as they studied the dark purple bruises on her swollen ankle.

"Might be broken," Devon said. "We need to take you to the hospital."

Dalton rested one arm behind her shoulders and scooped her legs into his brawny arms. She squealed at the unexpected movement.

"You don't have to carry me."

Being in his arms felt as natural as waking up. She leaned against his muscled chest before draping an arm around his shoulders. She could get used to him carrying her.

He snorted. "'Course I do. You're in no shape to walk."

Derin dropped the tailgate down, and Devon hopped in the back seat. Once Dalton guided her aching body into the back, Devon leaned over the seat and slung his arms under hers.

"Push with your good foot when I lift you," Devon said.

With little effort, he lifted River's upper body. She pushed against him until her rear and low back rested against the last row of seats. Then Dalton crawled next to her, despite there being a second row of seats. When he rested his arm around her shoulders, River snuggled against his chest, savoring his strength.

"Got anything else in the cabin?" Derin asked.

"My shirt and hat," she said.

He darted in and came right back out with River's and Dalton's shirts in one hand and their hats in the other.

"Here." He tossed the shirts to Dalton. "Roll them up to cushion that ankle."

Then he set the hats next to her before closing the tailgate. He climbed into the driver's seat. Devon handed them each a chilled water bottle.

"Drink up."

"How did you know where to find us?" River asked as Dalton's hand rubbed slow, fiery trails up and down her arm.

"The horses came back without you," Devon answered. "So Mami activated Dalton's 'find my phone.' It pointed to this area as his last location."

Dalton snorted. "For once, I'm glad that Mami spies on us."

"She does?" River asked, remembering their times in the hot tub. Heat warmed her cheeks.

"Not really. We all have that feature on our phones for this very reason."

When Derin hit a big rut, River closed her eyes and sucked in a sharp breath as waves of pain washed over her.

"Easy!" Dalton growled.

"Doin' my best D4."

"Here," Devon handed her an ibuprofen. "Might help, especially since you've got a long evening ahead of you."

"I'm not looking forward to hours of poking and prod-
ding at the hospital."

Dalton continued caressing her arm. "I know, but it's
necessary. I'm sure Chef has some leftovers we can eat on
the ride in."

They all went silent for the rest of the ride.

The moment Derin stopped the UTV by the dining hall,
a crowd of people rushed the vehicle.

"Mijo, are you hurt? Let me lay eyes on you," Catalina
greeted her son as soon as Devon dropped the tailgate.

"I'm fine, Mami. River hurt her ankle. We need to take
her—"

"*Mi rio bonita!*" Catalina placed a hand on River's cheek,
the motherly gesture endearing her to River even more. "We
will fix you up right away."

Dalton started, "Can I borrow—"

Tres tossed his truck keys to him. After unlocking the
vehicle, Dalton swooped her into his powerful arms. Arms
that had carried her away from a raging wash and across the
desert to the drover's cabin. She would always think of it as
theirs. The odd place where she first fell in love with him.
Maybe it was the pain messing with her brain. Or his closeness. It was too soon to fall in love with him.

"What did your mother call me?" she asked, trying to
stop thinking about what had changed between her and Dalton.

One side of his mouth quirked. "My pretty river."

She rested a hand over her heart as he helped her into
the passenger seat.

"Oh! How sweet. I love it."

"Mami!" Drake called. "Here are some sandwiches and
water. Take them with you."

"Gracias, mijo!"

Catalina climbed into the back seat behind Dalton while
he slid behind the wheel.

"Here, *rio bonita*. Eat." She thrust a roast beef sandwich

at River. Then she did the same to her son.

As River unwrapped the sandwich and bit off a chunk, Dalton told her not to rush.

"It'll take us about a half hour to get there."

"What happened?" Catalina asked from the back.

While Dalton explained, River's eyes fluttered closed. She would rest for a few minutes.

When the truck slowed, she opened her eyes. Dalton stopped it under a portico in front of the emergency room entrance. Catalina waved to an orderly for a wheelchair while Dalton exited the truck. He rounded to the passenger side and opened the door, quirking a saucy grin her way.

"One last time."

River snorted. "If I didn't know better, cowboy, I'd think you enjoy carrying me."

He shrugged. "Maybe just a little."

Once she was settled in the wheelchair, he turned away from her. She grabbed his arm. "Don't leave me here."

"Not a chance, *rio bonita*. I'll park the truck and come find you."

She let out a sweet sigh. She loved her new nickname. From his lips, it held promise and hope. Something she wanted to explore. Maybe tomorrow after she felt better.

The orderly wheeled her to the front desk, where a sympathetic woman handed her a stack of paperwork to fill out.

"Insurance?"

Crud. She should have stopped by her casita for her purse.

Catalina placed a hand on her shoulder. "Not to worry, *bonita*. I brought your purse."

"Oh, thank you."

River dug her wallet out of the large bag. She handed the card to the woman behind the counter. Then Catalina wheeled her over to the waiting area while she filled out the paperwork. Dalton's mom took the completed papers up to the desk and brought back her insurance card. A nurse called her name from nearby, so Catalina wheeled her behind the nurse.

The nurse helped River onto a bed and let her know the doctor would be in soon. She noticed the absence of odor in the room as she sank into the pillows. The softness felt comforting compared to the hard floor of the drover's cabin. Despite the throbbing in her foot, she felt like she could sleep for a week.

Dalton appeared in the doorway looking all mussed, masculine cowboy. Then he crossed the room in two strides. He leaned over her and placed a kiss on her forehead, sending wonderful ripples of warmth through her.

A few minutes later, a short Pakistani man in a white lab coat entered. The man's eyes darted from River to the cowboy standing next to the bed. It surprised River when the doctor greeted him first.

"Dalton, rough day at the ranch?" Lines formed near the corner of the doctor's eyes.

"You could say that. The monsoon storm rolled in and it stranded us for several hours. River's horse threw her and jacked up her ankle."

The doctor turned kind, dark eyes toward her as he extended his hand. "You must be River. Dr. Tahoor Aziz. Dalton and I go way back."

She offered him a wan smile.

Dr. Aziz's fingers gently prodded River's swollen ankle as he asked her a series of questions. He conducted a comprehensive assessment to determine if there were any other injuries caused by the fall. Then he ordered x-rays of her foot.

"It's been a busy evening, so it may be a half hour before the tech can get you in."

"Thank you, Dr. Aziz," she said before he left.

Dalton drew a chair nearer and gave her hand a reassuring squeeze. His gaze landed on her. "Tahoor is a skilled doctor. He'll fix you up."

She squeezed his hand, yawning. "I'm totally worn out."

"Well, skipping sleep, riding through a monsoon storm, and spraining your ankle could have something to do with that."

In a maternal tone, Catalina told River to rest while she waited.

River closed her eyes. She wasn't sure how much time had passed when the x-ray tech entered the room and took her back for the imaging. As much as she wished to have someone with her, she knew the tech wouldn't allow Catalina or Dalton back with her.

Instead, she prayed—for the first time since the storm. *Lord, please give Dr. Aziz wisdom to diagnose my injury. Thank you so much for Dalton and his amazing family. For them taking care of me and rescuing me. Thank you for the inspiration for my novel. Let this trip not be in vain.*

After the x-rays were taken, the tech wheeled her back to her room. Catalina sat on one side of her bed, Dalton on the other. She hoped to hear the results soon so she could go home and sleep for a week.

"When I heard the horses came back without you, I feared the worst," Mami said as soon as they wheeled River out of the hospital room for x-rays.

Dalton's mouth twisted downward. "Thank the Lord I spotted the drover's cabin. There was lightning and a huge dust storm. Without that shelter, things could have been much worse."

"Ay. *Alabado sea Dios.*" Mami raised her hands heavenward. He agreed. Praise be to God.

Then she turned her gold eyes on him. "She looks at you special, mijo."

"Mami," he warned, as heat flamed his face. His heart

sped up, hoping it was true.

"I see it. *Estar colado por*. Mad about you. Heart eyes. For you, mijo."

He saw it too. Felt it. Wanted it. Longed for it.

Except for one significant problem: River Sloane had a life on the other side of the country. She wouldn't stay long. After Janessa, he didn't have the heart to ask another woman to stay for him.

What could he offer her, anyway? A work-acholic husband who spent most of his time somewhere on the ranch. A meal and a few hours before he fell into bed weary, only to get up early and repeat it all the next day. He doubted that was the life River wanted.

The nurse wheeled his *rio bonita* into the room. As the nurse helped her back into the bed, she smiled at him. He didn't doubt her feelings. There was something strong and undeniable between them. He could practically touch its invisible force even then.

Tahoor knocked on the door, breaking Dalton's spinning thoughts. He caught the question in his friend's eyes. Even Tahoor noticed this thing between him and River. He fully expected a lunch invitation soon to talk about her.

"Good news, Miss Sloane. Your ankle is not broken."

River let out a loud breath. "Oh, good."

"The sprain is severe and will take time to heal."

When her shoulders drooped, Dalton didn't know whether to be happy or sad. Maybe she would have to stay at Vargas Ranch longer.

"A nurse will be in shortly to fit you for a boot and crutches. Then you'll be free to go. Keep it elevated as much as you can in the next forty-eight hours. Ice it too. Take anti-inflammatory medicine for the pain. Then follow up with an orthopedic surgeon sometime next week. They'll give you a better idea how long to wear the boot."

Dalton thanked his friend, then he hurried to pull the truck around. An orderly maneuvered River to the side of the truck in a wheelchair. Dalton lifted her into the passenger seat, laying the crutches in the back seat with his mother.

The drive back to the ranch took forever. Mami told him to bring River to the house. She insisted on fixing up one of his brother's old rooms for her. No doubt Mami would hover until River asked her to stop, or she felt better.

Once they arrived, he carried River into Derin's old room. Next to his. After he lowered her onto the edge of the bed, she reached for his hands.

"Thank you," she whispered.

He looked down into her hazel eyes, drowning in her, reluctant to leave her side.

"For rescuing me. Taking care of me."

Her mouth tilted in a half-smile and she tugged on his arm, drawing him closer. As he bent over her, she stretched up and placed a hand on his cheek. Followed closely by a brush of her soft lips on his. Just when he considered pulling her to her feet and into his arms for a deeper kiss, his mamacita cleared her throat from behind him.

"Renata brought some of your things."

Dalton stood to his full height. "*Dulces sueños, mi rio bonita.*"

She blinked and raised an eyebrow.

"Sweet dreams, my beautiful River," he whispered.

While pink bloomed on her cheeks, he turned and left the room, closing the door behind him. Walking to his room, he resolved to convince River to choose him and the ranch instead of her old life back in Ohio. *Foolish*, he thought as he stripped down and jumped into a steamy shower. He turned off the water and toweled off. Then he climbed into his bed.

Lord, is it possible that You brought River here for something more than inspiration for her novel? Could You have brought her for me? Is it selfish for me to want more?

Mami would say it wasn't selfish. She had already reminded him he could have a life. A wife. The thought caused an ache in his chest as big as a canyon. He wanted it more than he had realized.

Dalton flipped to his other side and jammed a pillow between his neck and shoulder. Thirty-four. Mami and Papi had been married and had five sons by his age. As the oldest, he figured he would marry first. Yet, with his luck, Dylan might beat him to the altar. That was unlikely. It would require Dylan to talk to a woman.

His mind raced through all the reasons he should stop thinking about River. Immediately, thoughts of winning her heart followed.

As the house quieted, he threw off the covers and padded into the dark kitchen. He reached for the fridge handle when a shadow startled him.

"Padre!" Dalton rested a hand over his throbbing heart.

"Dalton. Can't sleep?" The old man's voice held a touch of sympathy.

"Yeah," he answered as he flicked on the light over the stove.

"Me either. Hip is bothering me. I don't suppose yours is bothering you?"

The soft glint in Padre's eyes told Dalton he teased.

"Mine's more up here." He patted a hand over his heart.

"Your girl."

Dalton snorted. "She's not mine, Padre."

"But you want her to be."

Instead of answering, he retrieved a glass from the cupboard and pressed it against the filtered water dispenser in the fridge door. He gulped down half the glass before turning his attention to Padre.

"She reminds me of your grandmother."

"How so?"

"Elena rushed into my life faster and harder than a dust storm. One day she came to visit with her family. She smiled at me and I knew in a breath, she would become my wife."

He never knew his grandparents had a whirlwind romance. He handed Padre a glass of water and leaned against the cold, white quartz counter.

"From the first horse ride, she made it clear she liked me. Rode next to me. Stayed to help groom the horses after the ride, even though she was a guest. Invited me to sit by her at the firepit to toast marshmallows. One day, my life seemed full. The next, she breezed in and I realized how empty it had been. *She* made my life full."

"You must miss her terribly."

"I do. I proposed to her after knowing her for only two weeks."

Dalton's jaw slackened.

"I just knew. If you had asked me before Elena, if I believed in love at first sight, I'd have said no. Now? Absolutely."

Dalton doubted his situation was the same. "I... I don't think it's that way for me. I hardly know her."

"But you feel you've always known her."

It wasn't a question. A chill shimmied down his spine. Padre was right. Especially after their time in the drover's cabin. Those hours solidified whatever had sprouted in his heart the days before. River Sloane captivated him.

Padre yawned. Then he drained the glass and set it on the counter.

"Dalton, don't let your brain or some notion of how you think love is supposed to unfold get in your way. You're a planner and love sometimes doesn't follow anyone's plan."

"Yes, sir."

Dalton set the empty glasses by the sink. Then he offered to help Padre back to his room. He refused, so Dalton shuffled back to his own, more confused than before. Maybe daylight would bring clarity.

11

RIVER STRETCHED AND stopped short as the boot hit the side of her good leg. She wiped the sleepy sand from her eyes before she propped up on one arm. Light filtered in through the curtains, casting a glow over the unfamiliar room.

"Ay. River, let me help."

"Catalina, you don't have to—"

The sweet Mexican woman clucked her tongue and flicked her hand downward. Then she helped River sit up. River rested on the edge of the bed and straightened her sleep shorts and t-shirt before pushing off the bed. Catalina handed her the crutches.

"Let me go make you some breakfast. Or do you want lunch?"

"What time is it?"

"Almost eleven."

"Oh, my. I can't believe I slept so late."

"Don't worry, *bonita*. Dalton just woke up, too."

River's eyes widened. "Really?"

"Si. I made him promise to take it easy today. Of course, he's already locked himself in his office. Paperwork, no?"

River thanked her and said she would eat whatever the family was having. Then she donned her yellow sundress and slowly made her way to the large dining room. She kept her head down as she concentrated on using the crutches, their *click-clunk* echoing down the hallway. Her long hair hung forward, obscuring her vision.

"Want me to carry you again?"

She raised her head up at the sound of Dalton's deep voice. Then she snorted. "You seem a little too eager, cowboy."

He wrapped an arm around her waist and drew her close. She stilled at the familiar touch.

"Can you blame me?" he whispered in her ear. "Especially when you kissed me like that yesterday."

Heat spread across her face. He would bring up those kisses. Before she thought of a witty response, he swept her off her feet and into his arms. The crutches rattled as they hit the floor.

"Dalton!" she said his name with a broken laugh.

"You can admit you like when I carry you. I won't be shocked."

After he settled her onto a chair at the dining room table, he sat across from her.

"I heard you're playing hooky today."

His deep chuckle warmed her all the way to her toes. "Hardly. Catching up on paperwork is my least favorite part of the job."

"I suppose all my stuff is still at the casita. Maybe you could take me over?"

"Nope. Mami would have my hide. I can ask Renata to bring your things over."

She ducked her head. "I don't want to impose."

"Mami won't let you leave. Remember how I mentioned she spies on us boys?"

River bit her lower lip and nodded.

"Yeah, she's adopted you as one of her own, so she won't let you out of her sight until you're out of that boot."

"That could be weeks."

"I hope so."

The teasing left his eyes replaced with something stormy

that heated her cheeks. She got lost in his eyes for a moment, hoping right along with him.

"Oh, I need a new phone," she said, breaking the intensity of their connection.

"Me too. I'll head into town after lunch. Can I ask them to transfer your info to a new phone for you?"

"That would be nice."

Catalina cruised into the room with two heaping plates of tacos and a bottle of sriracha. Clearly, the latter was for Dalton and not her. Catalina smiled and sailed out of the room.

Dalton reached across the table to clasp River's hand. When he finished praying over the food, they both dug in.

"Mmm. This is delicious. They aren't tacos, are they?"

"Smoked pork carnitas. Probably the last of the meat Padre smoked."

"Sounds like you might have to ask him to teach you soon."

Dalton winked at her before he ate another bite. She could watch him all day long. Except as soon as the food filled her stomach, she felt sleepy again.

"You want me to carry you back to your room?" he teased.

"No, I can walk. I need to get used to the crutches."

River made it back to the room without his help. Catalina propped her leg up and placed ice on it for twenty minutes. By the time Catalina removed the ice, River's eyelids drifted shut, and she fell asleep.

DALTON GROANED AS he stretched, arms high overhead. Then he rubbed his eyes. He hated paperwork. At least it gave him an excuse to stay home, close enough to help if River needed anything.

He checked his phone. Still dead. Putting it in a bag of rice did nothing.

He stood and checked on River. She slept peacefully, her blond hair fanned around her head. The boot stuck out from the side of the covers. Her rosy lips were parted slightly. Even with her eyes closed, she looked lovely. His heart tugged as he watched her for a minute. Her ex had been a fool to let her get away. She was the most amazing woman.

Finally, he tore himself away from her and walked past the kitchen a second time. Mami called to him.

"I'll stay around and help her if she wakes up. *Vamos!*"

"Gracias, Mami."

Dalton drove to town to the cell phone store. After speaking at length with the owner, he purchased a replacement phone for himself and River. The store owner transferred the sim cards, and both powered on. Then he explained how to retrieve their contacts.

As Dalton sat in his truck with the AC on, he set up his phone. He had missed a message from Tahoor, so he texted him back. Tahoor messaged him he was on a break for an hour, so Dalton agreed to meet him at *The Lariat*.

When he entered the restaurant, Tahoor greeted him with a man hug before they both sat down.

"I ordered coffee for you."

"Thanks, bro."

"So, River, huh?" Tahoor asked, bright white teeth flashing in a grin.

Dalton sipped his black coffee, weighing how much to say. He and Tahoor had been friends since junior high school when Tahoor's father, also a doctor, moved the family to Wickenburg. They remained close friends even when Tahoor followed in his father's footsteps and went away to medical school. Most summers, his friend came out to the ranch and learned cowboying, too.

"Is she a guest?"

Dalton let out a long breath. Holding his friend's gaze,

he warned, "Keep this between us."

Tahoor nodded. "Of course."

"She's a romance writer. Kinda famous."

"And you like her?" Tahoor asked between bites of salad.

Dalton glanced away. "I shouldn't. She's gonna leave at the end of the month."

Tahoor snorted. "Not with that boot. I'll bet the orthopedic surgeon will keep her in it for six weeks or more."

Dalton smiled before he quickly masked it with a hearty gulp of coffee. He could only hope she would stay longer. Give him more time to win her heart.

"You've got it bad for her, don't you?"

He blew out a rushed breath. "Afraid so."

"It's about time you found a good woman."

Dalton frowned. "You match-making now?"

"No. But you aren't getting any younger. I just want you to be as happy as I am."

"You're lucky you found Shaima. She adores you."

"She puts up with my crazy schedule and is a great mom to the little ones. I was about ready to suggest you try the online dating thing."

"Not me, bro. Could never do that. Though I'm glad it worked out well for you."

They spent the next twenty minutes catching up. Tahoor shared pictures of his two little girls. Even though they all attended the local cowboy church together, Sundays were too rushed to talk for long.

By the time he left the coffee shop, it was almost time for dinner. Remembering River's favorite food, Dalton stopped by the Chinese restaurant and ordered beef lo mein and a few other dishes to go.

When he arrived at home, he set the food on the kitchen bar. Then he walked down the hall to River's room. He leaned against the doorway, crossing his arms over his chest. A smile tugged the corners of his mouth. She slept with one arm raised over her head. Her mouth hung open and soft snores reverberated in the room. She snorted and stirred right before her lovely hazel eyes popped open.

"Hey," she greeted him with a deep, sleep-laden tone that sent his pulse thrumming.

"Hungry?"

She sat up, swinging the heavy boot over the side of the bed.

"I could eat."

"Want me to carry you?"

She scrunched up her face with that expression he loved.

"No. I need to get used to using the crutches."

"Alright. I'll set out the food in the kitchen. Iced tea?"

She nodded as he handed her the crutches.

He waited a few seconds to make sure she didn't need more help, then he headed back to the kitchen. He opened all the Chinese food containers and grabbed a few plates. After pouring an iced tea for them both, he set the glasses at the bar.

Click. Clunk. Click. Clunk. The sound of the crutches echoed in the tile hallway.

"Smells good," River's voice sounded before she came into view.

As she rounded the corner, she halted. Moisture gathered in the corners of her eyes, causing his heart to squeeze tight.

"What's wrong?" he asked as he hurried to her side.

"Nothing." She snuffled. "You bought me lo mein."

The tightness in his chest loosened. "I thought it would make you feel better."

She hopped on her good foot until she faced him. "Come here."

Then he stepped closer, the crutches crashing to the floor as she wrapped her arms around his neck, her body pressing close. He enveloped her with his arms.

"You're the best," she whispered before she stood on her

tiptoes and drew his head down.

Then she kissed him. Sweet at first, those soft lips full of gratitude. He gently moved his mouth over hers, accepting every taste she allowed him, but not demanding more. When she pulled back, he loosened his hold, resting his cheek against the top of her silky hair. He breathed in the coconut scent of her shampoo.

"Thank you, Dalton. No one has ever brought me lo mein."

He chuckled. "Then how have you eaten it?"

"Okay. Only delivery drivers have brought it."

He slid his hand to the small of her back as she bounced on one foot toward the bar chair. Once she sat down, he picked up the crutches and leaned them against the counter nearby.

"What did you order?"

"Kung Pao. Extra spicy."

River giggled. "Why am I not surprised?"

"There's some almond honey chicken, egg rolls, and fried pot stickers, too."

Before he sat next to her, he drew her new phone from his pocket and slid it across the countertop.

Wide hazel eyes lit with excitement. "You got me a new phone, too?"

He winked at her as she beamed.

"You win boyfriend of the year award."

The breath lodged in his chest. His pulse raced as he studied her face. Had she meant it?

"Let's eat," she said.

He cleared his throat. "Wait. Do you mean that?"

Her eyes darted to the food and back to him. "That I'm hungry?"

"No. Boyfriend." His pulse thrummed loudly in his ears as he waited for her answer.

She reached up and placed a hand on his cheek. "Just calling it like I see it, Dalton. Does it bother you?"

He shook his head. "Not at all. I like it. A lot."

"Good. Now, can we pray and eat? I'm starving."

Dalton clasped his girlfriend's hand. Girlfriend. It felt right to think of his *rio bonita* that way. Then he led them in a prayer before they dished up the food.

"Where is everyone else?" she asked between bites of her lo mein.

"Probably at the dining hall." He swallowed a mouthful of kung pao chicken. "Renata brought the rest of your things over. Mami said you should stay with us until you're out of that boot."

"If you're sure. I don't want to impose."

"We can set up a desk for you to write. Pick a place."

"Hmm. That might be hard. I mean, the house is so small."

He laughed. He loved the way she injected humor into almost every conversation. "I'm sure you'll find *somewhere* in the six thousand square feet of the house."

She rolled her eyes. "If I must."

Then her joviality disappeared as a frown flickered on her face. "Did you ever figure out whose drone that was?"

It took him a second to track her abrupt change of subject. "The one that followed us?"

"Yeah."

"Sorry, I forgot about it. My girlfriend sprained her ankle and all."

River snorted. "I guess I'll forgive you. After all, you brought me lo mein."

"I'll look into it, though."

They talked and picked at the Chinese food, losing track of time. At last, River reminded him she needed to elevate her foot and ice it. He helped her onto the couch in the living room. Then he retrieved the ice pack and removed the boot. Everything about the evening felt like it was exactly how his life should be. Day in and day out. Her. There.

Please Lord. Let her want to stay.

Once River retired to her room for the night, Dalton headed over to the bunkhouse to talk to Derin.

"Hey, got your text. What's this about a drone?" Derin asked.

"When we were riding along Verde Wash, I spotted a drone. It wasn't one of ours."

"You were there at noon?"

"Yeah. Not the right time of day for hikers. Didn't seem like BLM either."

Derin rubbed a hand over his short beard.

"She mentioned something about a stalker, but —"

"A stalker!"

"Shh! Keep your voice down." Dalton glanced around the room. The cowboys and his other brothers returned their attention to a card game.

"She told me about this guy back in Columbus that might be following her. But she doesn't think he would know about her trip here."

"Still, we should be vigilant."

"Agreed."

"I'll ask around. Want to bring the security guard back early before the fall season starts?" Derin asked.

"I'm not sure. Do what you think is best."

Derin gave a curt nod in response.

Dalton didn't know if it could be the stalker or someone else. One thing was certain, he would be sure to take River wherever she needed to go into town or to medical appointments until he got to the bottom of it.

12

ON MONDAY MORNING, River accepted Dalton's offer for a ride to the doctor's office. She had called an orthopedic surgeon on Friday and they put her on a wait list. Thankfully, they called with an opening.

The front desk clerk greeted her and took down her information. Then Dalton walked beside her until she found a seat in the waiting area. When his phone rang, he apologized and took the call outside in the heat. She felt bad for keeping him away from his work.

A half hour later, a nurse led her down a hallway to an exam room. After checking her vitals, she verified they had received the records from the hospital. A few minutes later, the doctor entered the room, a kindly man with a crooked smile.

"Miss Sloane," Dr. Gregson greeted her. "So, a horse threw you in a monsoon storm?"

"Yeah."

"I'm sure the hospital told you there are no broken bones. Let's take the boot off and have a look."

River bent down and removed the bulky boot and her sport sock. The purple bruises had faded to a greenish yellow-brown. When Dr. Gregson pressed on the top of her foot, near the bruises, she sucked in a sharp breath.

"Hmm. May have some ligament damage here."

She slouched at the news. That couldn't be good.

He continued pressing on different areas of her foot and ankle before sharing the prognosis.

"It's definitely a severe sprain with a possible ligament tear. The swelling appears under control. Keep the boot on except for icing your foot and showering. I want to check your progress again in six weeks."

"Six weeks? But I'm due to fly back to Ohio at the end of the month."

"If you can delay your travel plans, that might be wise. If not, you'll want to follow up with an orthopedic surgeon there."

River bit her lower lip as she donned her sock and boot. Then she plodded down the hallway on her crutches.

She was torn. She should want to go home. Yet, the ranch, Dalton, and the Vargases felt like home in a way her apartment in Columbus never had. She had what she needed with her, so she could write her novel at the ranch. They weren't charging her to stay in the house. Staying would give her more time with Dalton and to learn about ranching.

At the front desk, she scheduled the followup appointment for the middle of August.

On the ride back, she remained quiet. Dalton took a business call, so he hadn't asked about what the doctor said. She was glad because she still needed time to decide what she would do. Stay or go home as planned?

Back at the ranch, Dalton helped her up the porch stairs before he left to deal with some issues at the tennis court construction site.

Once in the solitude of her bedroom, she called her mom and explained the situation.

"Oh, honey. The Vargases sound wonderful. I think you should stay. You can write from anywhere. There's no need to rush back here. Besides, it sounds like you may have found someone special."

She sighed dreamily. "Dalton is special. I like him a lot, Mom."

"That settles it. As long as they will have you, you should stay."

After River hung up, she tramped down to her temporary office—Devon's old room. She propped the crutches against the wall and eased into the office chair. Once her laptop booted up, she opened her manuscript and wrote.

Scenes flowed quickly from the keyboard onto her screen. Her hero finally admitted he didn't allow others to get close, especially since the tragic plane accident that robbed him of loving parents. Her heroine's heart softened. She told him about her abusive ex and how she escaped with their son. A closeness developed between them.

River sighed as she sipped an iced tea that Catalina had dropped off earlier. Writing cowboy romance wasn't bad. It shared many of the same elements of her other novels. Different setting. Different jobs and day-to-day activities. Honestly, she kind of enjoyed writing fresh scenarios to bring her characters closer.

After a few hours, she turned her attention to planning Dalton's association's website. She would meet with Solana soon. She couldn't wait until she finished it. Dalton would love it. And she felt good about doing this one thing for him.

DALTON WISHED HE could take the day off or even another hour to catch up with River. Unfortunately, an issue with the construction site required his immediate attention. He still needed to drive back into town to buy a birthday gift for River. He intended to do that during her appointment, but a long call kept him busy until her appointment finished.

After lifting his hat, he ran a hand through his hair before plopping it back down. His phone rang again.

"Yeah?"

"We have a problem," Derin said.

Of course, they had a problem. When did they not? That was the only reason anyone ever called him.

"Someone cut the fence on the north pasture."

Dalton growled. "So fix it."

"Hey, don't shoot the messenger. Just thought you'd want to know why we're paying everyone overtime for today. Got to round up the missing cattle and fix the fence."

"Got it."

Dalton lowered his phone but heard Derin still jabbering.

"Was there something else?" he asked as he pressed it against his ear again.

"I asked if the pyro guys came by? I was supposed to meet with them regarding the fireworks, but I've been stuck out here all day."

"Let me find out."

He ended the call and he rang Renata.

"You heard from the fireworks guys?"

"Yeah. They're all set for tomorrow."

"Bless you, cuz."

He texted Derin they were all set.

His phone rang again.

"Yeah?"

"Don't sound so chipper," Drake said.

"On a tight schedule." He yanked his truck door open and climbed behind the wheel.

"We have an order at the restaurant supply store that needs picked up, but I'm helping Chef with some of the prep work for tomorrow."

"See if Devon—"

"He's helping set up for tomorrow."

"What about Dylan?"

"Sick mare. He's waiting for the vet to show."

"Text me the address. How much are we talking? Will it fit in my truck?"

"It'll fit. I think."

The line went dead. Then the address popped up in his messages. He clicked on the address while his truck engine growled awake. Punching the AC to full blast, he backed out and headed into Wickenburg.

Drake texted him again. *They close in forty.*

How was he supposed to shop for a gift for River when he barely had enough time to pick up the order of food? It's not like he could leave the food sitting out in one hundred and ten degree temps.

He asked his smart phone to call Mami.

"Mijo! What's going on?"

"Mami, I'm in a jam. I have to go pick up a food order and bring it straight back, but I haven't gotten to the jewelry store yet."

"What do you need at the jewelry store?"

"A birthday gift for River."

"Already?" His mother squealed in delight.

"Mami, it's not a ring." Too soon for that.

"I know, mijo. But jewelry is pretty serious, no?"

He expelled an exasperated breath.

"I really wanted to pick out something special, but I'm out of time. They'll be closed by the time I could make it back to town. I need other ideas."

"Ay. You know we sell some pretty jewelry in the gift shop. Just ask Renata when you get back. I'm sure you can find something she'd like."

"Gracias, Mami."

He hung up and drummed his fingers on the steering wheel, while stuck behind a slow car on the two-lane highway. He really hoped they had something nice in stock at the gift shop. The last thing he wanted to do was mess up his girlfriend's birthday.

A smile twitched at the corners of his mouth. He enjoyed calling River his girlfriend. She was everything he wanted in a woman. Gorgeous. Smart. Adventurous. Funny. He couldn't believe it had been almost two weeks since he rescued her from the Safeway parking lot. It felt like he had known her for months.

The slow car in front of him turned onto a side road, so Dalton punched the accelerator until he hit the town limits. Right at the forty-minute mark, he pulled up to the dock in the back of the store. A middle-aged balding man motioned him to stop. Then he dropped his tailgate, and the man wheeled several tall stacks of boxes into the back.

Dalton frowned as he dug some tie down bungees and straps from his toolbox before they started stacking stuff on top of it. His truck could haul a lot, but this had to be over the weight limit. He wasn't too sure about the stability of the cargo, either. The load obscured his rear view too.

The balding man helped him secure everything with the tie downs. The tires on his truck bowed under the weight. Not exactly safe.

"Thanks!" he tossed over his shoulder before he drove away.

Through town, he took turns slowly, nervously watching the stack of boxes for any shifting. So far, so good. Once he reached the highway, he kept his speed down. About four miles from his turnoff, he heard the loud pop followed by the *thud, thud, thud* of a shredded tire. The steering wheel vibrated violently as he eased the wobbly truck to the side of the road. He asked his smart phone to dial Drake.

"Hey, this is Drake. Leave a message."

"Bro. I'm stranded on the side of the road with your load. Bring a truck and trailer. There's too much weight for the bed of a pickup truck."

After leaving the message, he called Renata and told her the same. She said she would get someone to come right away.

Right away ended up being a half hour later. He sure hoped none of the food spoiled. He hated wasting money like that.

Devon and Drake pulled up behind him with a trailer.

The pungent smell of sun-warmed asphalt hung heavy in the air. As Dalton hefted two boxes from his truck, sweat trailed down his back. Humidity thickened the air. The three of them spent the next forty minutes transferring one or two boxes at a time to the trailer. By the time they finished, his stomach growled, and he still needed to swap out his blown tire.

"Here's some water. You want me to stay to help?" Drake asked.

"No. You best get that food out of here and out of the heat."

"Okay. If you have any trouble, ring Papi. He can help."

Right. Like he would ask his fifty-six-year-old father to stand in the brutal heat to help him change a tire. He saluted his brothers as they pulled away. At least they brought him some water.

Another half hour later, weary and hungry, Dalton finally pulled away from the side of the road. By the time he made it back to the resort, the dining hall had closed. Renata was already gone for the day. So he drove to the ranch house where Mami surely had food for him.

When Dalton opened the back door, his mother called for him.

"Yes, Mami?"

"I'll heat some tamales and rice."

He nodded and turned on his heel.

"Mijo, wait."

She walked across the kitchen and pressed a small velvet box into his hand. "If you don't like it, then we'll get something else."

"Gracias, Mami."

Then he hurried down the hall to his room. Once inside, he opened the jewelry box and his eyes burned. It was exactly what he would have picked for River. His mamacita knew him so well. It was perfect.

After a quick splash in the shower, he donned fresh

shorts and a t-shirt before returning to the kitchen. His mouth watered when he smelled the tamales and rice.

"Hey."

There River sat, looking all beautiful and comforting. Best sight ever.

"Rough day?"

"To put it mildly."

She patted the bar stool next to her. Dalton bent down to kiss her cheek, but she turned her face at the last minute, surprising him with a delicious kiss. When he ended it, he rested his forehead against hers.

"I could get used to dessert before dinner." His voice sounded thick with emotion.

River grinned and swatted at his arm. "Eat while I tell you some good news."

He sat and bowed his head, offering a prayer for her and for the food. As soon as he said "Amen," his phone rang again.

"One sec." He held up a finger to her as he answered it, his annoyance rising.

"D4. We found all but six head," Derin said. "We'll look again at daybreak."

Dalton frowned. "Thanks for letting me know. If you know which tags, text me."

"You got it, boss."

He plunked his phone on the counter and closed his eyes. Six wasn't the end of the world. No. All the chaos of the day ate at him. A soft hand rested on his forearm.

"Tell me about your day."

"No. You tell me your news while I eat."

"Okay, but I still want to hear about your day when you're finished."

He nodded and scraped the husk off his tamales before liberally dashing them with sriracha.

"The doctor said…"

He had completely forgotten about her appointment. It

felt like three days ago with all that happened.

"He said I might have a torn ligament. I need to wear the boot for at least six weeks."

Dalton chewed slower. She was due back in Ohio in four weeks.

"After talking it over with Tres and Catalina, we all agree that I can stay here as long as I need to recover."

His heart slammed against his chest. Dare he hope?

"I'm going to stay through the end of August. At the very least."

After swallowing the burning bite of tamale, he angled toward her. "Eight weeks?"

"At a minimum."

A minimum. His heart rammed against his chest. Did she want to stay longer? Forever?

He best not get ahead of himself. He would take the eight weeks. More if she would give it.

"And you can write here?"

"Already am. All I need is internet."

Slowly, a grin spread across his face. He stood and pulled her into his arms, rocking her back and forth, burying his nose in her hair. Her familiar floral scent felt like home.

"I take it you're happy?"

"Ecstatic. Joyful. Blessed."

"Okay, okay. Put me down and finish your meal. Tell me all about your day."

"Well, it was rough. But it ended with the best news I've heard in years."

River giggled. "I'm serious, Dalton. Tell me about the rough part, too."

In between bites of tamales and rice, he told her all about it. As the time passed, his burden lifted, replaced with the joy that his *rio bonita* would stay longer.

13

———

"*MI RIO BONITA*!" Catalina's sing-song voice pulled River from sleep. "Happy Birthday!"

River scooted to sit upright in bed as Catalina entered the room. She carried a tray of mouth-watering food and a small vase with one red rose. After she helped River take off the boot, Catalina set the tray over her lap and laid an ice pack on her ankle.

"Enjoy! I'll be back in fifteen minutes for the ice."

"Wait!" River called, but Catalina buzzed away like a busy bee.

"Morning," Dalton said as he entered her room. "I see you got my first gift."

River snorted. "I don't believe for one minute that you made any of this."

"Oh, I didn't. But I picked the rose just for you."

Butterflies fluttered in her tummy over his thoughtfulness and steady gaze. When he tried to snag a piece of bacon, she shooed him away from her food. She expected him to say his farewells and leave, so it surprised her when he sat in the overstuffed chair. A gentle smile spread across his handsome face.

"Don't you have cows to count or brothers to boss?"

Dalton chuckled for several seconds. "Cows to count. Love it."

She smiled around a bite of *huevos rancheros*, an egg dish

that quickly had become her favorite breakfast.

"I'm easing into the day." He raised his coffee mug before sipping it.

"And you wanted a good laugh? I'm sure my hair is a wreck and I probably have lines on my face or drool on my shirt."

"You look perfect." His husky voice sent thrilling tremors up her spine.

"So, what are your plans for the day?" she asked, before sipping the orange juice.

"First, I'm gonna watch my girlfriend eat breakfast in bed. I could get used to such beautiful scenery in the morning." He winked at her.

Heat flamed her cheeks. She didn't mind staring at his ruggedly handsome face first thing, either.

"Then I'm going to head over to the dining hall to make sure Drake has everything ready for the day. After the snafu with the food order yesterday, he's on a short leash."

"Was that his fault?"

"Not really, but I'm grooming him to run the dining hall and coffee shop. It's too much on Renata's plate and he's got a stake in our entire operation. She doesn't. Won't hurt him to step up more."

"And after you've given him a hard time?"

"I'll probably ride out to the north pasture to inspect the repaired fence and to see if Derin found the missing cattle. Then I'll come back, shower, and watch my girlfriend write a romance novel. Maybe kiss her a few times to inspire her. Who knows?"

Again, her face warmed with his teasing. She liked his plan. Especially the kissing part.

"What else?"

"I think the time with my girlfriend is going to eat up my afternoon. Probably my evening too. After all, it's her birthday and I want her to feel special."

"She does like feeling special. And she enjoys delightful

surprises. Like breakfast in bed. Tell me, was that Catalina's idea or yours?"

"My idea. Her food. I don't make very good *huevos rancheros.*"

"Any other plans?"

"Once the sun goes down, I'm gonna drive my girlfriend over to the firepit to watch this amazing fireworks show put on by Vargas Guest Ranch & Resort. I've heard people come from all over the area to see it and I secured front row seats, including an extra chair for one booted foot."

"Mmm. Sounds perfect."

"Just as perfect as my *rio bonita.*"

River's cheeks flushed again. She gulped the last of her orange juice and patted the cloth napkin on her lips.

"All done?"

When she nodded, Dalton stood and moved the tray for her. He grabbed the ice pack with his other hand. Then he stood in the doorway.

"See you this afternoon. And be ready for some serious kissing."

River laughed as he left.

She stretched her arms above her head before gathering her clothes and toiletries. Then she showered, dressed, and hobbled to her office.

As she sat down to write, she said a quick prayer, thanking God for bringing her to Vargas Ranch. And for making a way for her to stay longer.

Then she turned on her laptop, popped in ear buds, and played some high energy music. Words flowed from her mind. The story came to life in glorious detail. Personalities solidified. The music poured into the emotions of the characters. She closed her eyes as her fingers flew across the keyboard. She could see what they saw. Smell the fresh air of the Arizona ranch. The sun beat down on them, warming their skin. Cattle plodded along. The hero had eyes only for her.

Just like her Dalton.

River's heart skipped a beat. She couldn't leave him. Not in eight weeks or eight months or eight years. Her eyes flew open as the realization rooted in her heart.

But she had a life in Ohio. A life that no longer held any appeal.

Focus, River. The book.

Right. She reread the last scene and progressed the story forward.

A few hours later, still in the zone, the warmth of a hand rested on her shoulder. She screamed and spun around while ripping the ear buds from her ears.

"Sorry," Dalton said. "Didn't realize you were listening to something."

River rested a hand over her chest as she struggled to slow her heart rate and breathing.

"You scared the daylights out of me."

"Bad time?"

She blew out a rush of air. "No. I'm overdue for a break."

Dalton turned her to face him. Then he lifted her to her good foot and wrapped her in his powerful arms. "I always keep my promises."

His warm lips captured hers for several sweet kisses, increasing in intensity. After a few minutes, she ended the kisses.

"Do you need to write more?" he asked.

"No, I'm done for the day. Let me shut this down."

"I'll fix you a snack. Join me in the kitchen when you're ready." He trailed his calloused fingers down the side of her face, neck, and arm before he left the room, causing her heart to sing.

A few minutes later, she shuffled on her crutches into the kitchen. A small wrapped box sat on the bar next to a plate of cheese and meat. He helped her to a seat and propped the crutches against the counter.

"Happy Birthday."

With bright eyes and an eager expression, he slid the small box toward her. River's pulse danced as jitters started in her stomach. She untied the ribbon, setting it aside. Then she tore off the cute cupcake paper to reveal a blue velvet box. Her breath caught as her gaze jumped to his. He gave her an encouraging nod.

The little box creaked as she opened it. A white gold necklace rested on the black satin pillow inside the box. Her eyes burned.

"I love it," she whispered as she ran her thumb over the Vargas Ranch brand hanging from a delicate chain.

"I will not deviate from the Lord's plan," she whispered.

Dalton's eyes softened with his sweet smile.

"Will you put it on me?"

He slipped the necklace from the jewelry box before standing behind her. She held her hair to the side. Once he secured the clasp, he placed a soft kiss on the side of her neck. A hum rose in her throat as she closed her eyes and savored the sensation. His fingers left trails of fire behind as he ran them across her shoulders. But he didn't linger.

As he sat on the bar stool next to her, she fingered the necklace. She would wear it often.

"This is so nice, Dalton."

"So you like it then?"

"I love it. And I love you."

The unexpected words hung in the air. She hadn't meant to say them. But her heart wouldn't allow her to deny it any longer. She loved this real cowboy, so much better in the flesh than any character she could dream up. He was real. Kind. Caring. And incredibly handsome. A man of character. Honor.

River leaned over and kissed him on the cheek. Then she sat back and popped a bite of cheese into her mouth. His eyes remained fixed on hers for several seconds.

DALTON CLEARED HIS throat. "I love you, too, *rio bonita*."

Warmth expanded his chest with the admission. Words he had been afraid to say. Yet now that he voiced them, they seemed both heartfelt and frightening. He had done it. He gave River Sloane his heart. In two glorious weeks.

Hopefully, it wasn't foolish.

He swiped a piece of cheese from the plate and ate it. She smiled at him, sending his stomach quivering.

When she pushed the plate away, he wrapped it with plastic and placed it in the fridge. After he handed her the crutches, he carried their beverages into the living room. He sat on one side of the couch, and she sat next to him. She leaned against him as she swung her legs onto the cushions. He rested his arms around her, stroking her silky golden hair.

They snuggled together for a long time, talking about anything and everything. If every evening of the rest of his life ended like this, he would be a blessed man.

As the sun ducked behind Dalton Peak, he led her out to the truck. When she settled in the passenger side, he rounded the truck. He paused as he heard a distant humming. His eyes searched the sky. Sure enough, a drone hovered overhead.

Dalton frowned. He unlocked his toolbox and retrieved his rifle. After siting in the drone, he saw enough of it to confirm it wasn't Vargas-owned. He stowed his rifle, still unwilling to shoot the thing down. Could be someone getting ready to record the fireworks show.

As he slid into the driver's seat, River asked, "What's wrong?"

"The drone is back."

"Not yours?"

He shook his head as he turned the ignition. The truck

revved to life, and he drove them over to the dining hall. He tried to put the drone out of his mind as they entered the lodge.

People packed the place. Every table was filled. Good for business. Not so good for River's foot.

"Dalton!" Devon waved him over.

River followed behind at a good pace. She expertly navigated through the crowd with the crutches.

"Here, River, take my seat. I just finished." He stood, plate in hand, shoveling the last few bites into his mouth.

River thanked him and eased into the chair.

Dalton left her at the table and filled a plate for her before he returned to the line for his own meal. By the time he joined River, someone had vacated the chair next to her.

"I can't believe there are so many people here."

He chuckled. "I told you people come from all over for the fireworks."

"And you invited them all to my birthday."

He snickered at her joke.

As soon as they finished eating, he walked next to River to the chairs he had set up for them near the firepit. Tonight, there would be no fire in the pit. Instead, he and his brothers filled the pit with flameless battery-powered candles — Renata's idea. All the ambiance without the heat, she said.

Folks set out lawn chairs behind them, facing the gravel lot on the other side of the firepit. During peak season, they used the area for staging trail rides. No grass nearby to catch fire from the fireworks. They took many precautions to reduce any risk of accidental fires.

Dusk faded to night. Stars sparkled across the dark sky. Derin stood near the firepit and announced the opening of the twenty-sixth annual Vargas Ranch fireworks display. Patriotic music emanated from the speakers as the crowd hushed and looked toward the sky.

Dalton rested his arm over River's shoulder after scooting his chair closer. She released a soft breath and leaned into him. He had never watched the fireworks with a girl-friend before.

The first few flares screamed into the air. Bursts of white faded to blue.

"Oh!"

Her joy caused a smile to spread across his face. He glanced at her. The red fireworks cast glowing color over her pale skin and the necklace shimmered. A soft smile stretched across her lips.

"Thanks for the birthday fireworks," she whispered as she jabbed her elbow in his ribs.

"Anytime."

After placing a kiss on her temple, he turned his attention back to their best show yet. The explosions of light shone against the starry sky, matching the mood of the music perfectly. He would tell Derin how great it turned out. His brother had done an amazing job, and Dalton planned to put him in charge of it going forward.

When the music faded and the night cocooned them in its warmth, he shifted slightly. River looked up at him and he landed a heated kiss on her lips, lodging his fingers in her silky locks. She parted her warm lips, inviting him to lose himself as her floral fragrance filled his senses. Love for her overwhelmed him, causing him to forget the surrounding crowd.

A loud buzzing sounded too close. His pulsed raced, partly from the kiss and partly from adrenaline warning him of danger. He tore away from River, launching to his feet.

"D4!" Derin called out. "That ain't ours."

He told River he would be back shortly before he jogged over to his brother.

"It's the same one I saw earlier today. Same as the day we were caught in the monsoon."

"Seems to be everywhere you are."

River.

"You mean wherever River is."

"What can we do about it?" Derin asked.

"Dunno," Dalton replied. The thought of shooting it down niggled in the back of his mind. Still didn't seem like the right thing to do.

"Isn't there some law about flying over private property?"

"Yeah, but we'd have to catch whoever is doing it. They must be close by."

"I'll get a few of the boys and we'll see if we can't find them. Though in this crowd, it's gonna be hard."

"Thanks. I'm gonna take River into the dining hall."

"We'll meet up later."

"Dalton!" River called his name, fear evident in her tone.

When he rushed to her, she turned her phone for him to see. His gut twisted tight. The picture showed him passionately kissing River. Just a half hour ago.

"He has my number. He texted it to me."

His blood burned. River's stalker just escalated, and he aimed to put an end to it.

"I'm calling the sheriff," he said as he yanked his phone from his pocket.

The dispatcher said it would be a few hours before they could send someone out. Unfortunately, living on the northwest corner of Maricopa County put them far from the sheriff's office. Wickenburg was the closest station.

Dalton told the dispatcher to send the deputy to the ranch house when he arrived. Then he drove River home.

Back at the ranch house, he grabbed his laptop and sat with River on the couch. He pulled up the security feeds for the night, and they both reviewed them.

"Let me know if anyone looks familiar."

By the time the sheriff's deputy arrived, they had gone through several hours of footage. Nothing stood out. His brothers and the other cowboys found little.

"Do you have a picture of the drone or the operator?" the deputy asked.

"I do," Derin said, as he burst through the door, looking fierce.

Dalton held his breath. The picture of the operator was clear.

"I wasn't able to stop him, but I snapped a picture. Got his license plate too, but it looks like a rental car."

River asked to see the picture. Her face went white as she stared at it. Dalton tightened his arm around her, as if he could do anything to help her feel safe again.

"That's him. How does he know I'm here?"

"You know this man?" the deputy asked, taking notes.

"Yes. I live in Ohio, and I kept running into him in various places. The grocery store. Coffee shop."

"Do you know his name?"

She shook her head. "I wasn't sure if he was a threat or not. He asked me how I was. Commented on the weather. Never tried to touch me. Never asked for anything. So I thought he was harmless."

"What can we do?" Dalton asked.

"I'll submit these pictures to the FAA as a complaint. If you feel threatened by the drone or the operator, then you can defend yourself. I'll also contact the rental car company to see if I can find any information on him."

"That's it?" Dalton asked gruffly.

"I'm afraid there's not much I can do besides investigate it and write up a report. Unless we catch him in the act."

Dalton rubbed his hand on River's arm as she pushed into his side. He didn't like the deputy's answer. The deputy asked for copies of all the photos, including the one the stalker sent to River.

Derin showed the deputy out before returning to the living room. "I'm gonna bring security back through the rest of the summer."

"Sounds good."

"If we see it again, I say we shoot it down. Fines be—"

"It's not an easy target," Dalton said. "The last thing we

need is a stray bullet on the property."

Derin growled. "It's not right. We should be able to do something."

"Let's look up more about the model. Its battery life, range, etc. Maybe it'll help us figure out how to catch the guy."

"Fine. I'll do some research and send out an employee wide text."

"Thanks, Derin."

As soon as everyone left, River turned to him. "Do you think he'll try to hurt me?"

Dalton let out a slow breath. "I don't know. He said nothing in the text. Just sent the picture."

She rested her head on his chest, and he stroked her hair.

"Just make sure you're with one of us wherever you go on the property."

"Okay."

Lord, please keep her safe. Give us wisdom about how to deal with this threat.

Despite the prayer, his throat tightened. He hated the situation. He wanted to keep her safe. Only, in this case, he didn't know how.

14

TWO WEEKS LATER, River plotted with Catalina to give Dalton a day off. River was up and ready before he appeared for breakfast.

"Morning," she greeted him with a smile and a black coffee, just the way he liked it.

"Morning. You're up early."

"I'm kidnapping you for the day." She flashed him a big grin.

Dalton's eyes traveled down to her booted foot. "And how do you propose to do that?"

"Well, it won't be easy. I need a chaufer."

She closed the space between them and balanced her crutches against the kitchen bar. Then she rested her arms behind his neck. "I thought maybe I could convince you to drive."

As he wrapped his arms around her, he asked, "And where are we going?"

"It's a surprise."

He laughed and cute lines crinkled near his eyes. "If I'm the driver, I'm gonna need to know where we're going."

"Well, when you come back here at nine, I'll let you know. Don't be late."

"Alright."

Dalton leaned down and gave her a toe-curling kiss. Slowly, he released her. He rested his forehead against hers.

"I could get used to morning kisses like this."

"Mmm. Me too."

After a minute, he released her.

"Nine o'clock. Don't be late, cowboy."

"Yes, ma'am."

River smiled as he turned and waved to her from the front door. She shuffled down the hall toward her office. She spent the next few hours working on her book. Memories from the cabin inspired the romance scenes. Finally, at a quarter til nine, she shut down her computer, grabbed her purse, and waited for Dalton.

When he pulled his truck to a stop, she opened the front door and hopped toward the porch stairs. He jumped out of his truck.

"Hang on!"

In two strides, he was by her side, swooping her into his arms. He carried her down the stairs and settled her in the passenger side, stealing another kiss. A saucy grin turned up one side of his mouth.

"I've been thinking about you all morning."

River giggled. "Good. One more thing before we go."

"Yeah?"

"You'll need to put that cooler in the back. We have multiple stops to make."

Dalton laid her crutches in the back seat and retrieved the cooler. He placed it on the floor behind her seat before sliding into the driver's side.

"Where to, *rio bonita*?"

She asked for his phone and typed in the address for their first stop. She secured his phone to his hands-free holder.

"No peeking," she warned. "Just follow the navigation instructions."

Dalton laughed. "You really do like surprises, don't you?"

River smiled. "Roll out, cowboy!"

His chuckle warmed her heart. She loved this man. Couldn't picture leaving him. Ever. She sure hoped he enjoyed her surprise as much as she thought he would.

As he eased off the highway and drove down a street in Wickenburg, he chuckled again. "The butcher?"

She gasped, marginally disappointed he had figured it out. "How did you know? We're still a few blocks away."

"I've lived here my whole life, River. It's the only place I can think of in this direction."

Her shoulders sagged. "I hadn't thought about that."

Dalton reached over and clasped her hand with his. "I still don't know why you're taking me to the butcher."

"Padre is going to teach you how to smoke ribs this afternoon. He said if we get back in time, he'll teach you carnitas as well."

As he placed his hand back on the steering wheel, she noticed her rugged cowboy swallowing a few times.

"That is." He coughed. "A wonderful surprise."

"I thought you'd like it. Padre is really looking forward to it. He did not know you wanted to learn and was tickled when I told him. I hope you don't mind me sharing that secret."

"You're something else, *rio bonita.*"

When he pulled the truck to a stop in front of the butcher, he cut the engine. Then he angled toward her. His eyes studied hers for a few seconds as he held her hands.

He opened his mouth a few times, but no words came. At last, he released her hands and exited the truck. He helped her down and handed her the crutches. Leaving him speechless hadn't been her goal. It pleased her she picked the perfect surprise for him.

"I suppose that's what the cooler is for."

"Yeah. We'll need to buy some ice for it too. We have another stop to make that might take an hour or more."

He held the door of the shop open. The owner greeted them.

"What can I do for you, Dalton?"

"Need some ribs and—"

"Padre said we should get ten slabs of baby back ribs and thirty pounds of pork shoulder. Boneless, if you have it."

"Sure thing, miss."

"River Sloane," Dalton introduced her to Scott, the butcher.

"You said Junior sent you in?" Scott asked.

"Yeah."

"He normally picks up a few briskets while he's in. Do you want me to wrap up some?"

Dalton looked at River and raised an eyebrow.

"He said none today. Not enough time to smoke it this afternoon."

"Tell him I said we miss seeing his ornery hide around here."

River laughed. "Next time we'll bring him with us."

NEXT TIME.

The words rang in Dalton's ears. He could picture bringing Padre with them. Many times. For years to come. He would enjoy the outing and Dalton would enjoy bringing River with him.

His *rio bonita* planned all this for him. An afternoon with Padre, learning to smoke ribs and carnitas. Something he had casually mentioned in the drover's cabin. Yet, she remembered and orchestrated this day just for him. He could scarcely believe it.

Once Scott finished wrapping their order, Dalton pulled out his wallet. River placed a hand on his arm.

"This one is my treat. You can pay for the next surprise."

He felt awkward letting her pay, but she insisted. The

price was more than he expected, but she didn't bat an eye. He lifted all the bags off the counter and held the door open for River. She told Scott it was a pleasure meeting him after all the good things Padre told her.

Dalton couldn't help wondering just when she came up with this idea. Clearly, she had talked with Padre at length about this. After he placed the meat and ice in the cooler, he asked her where their next destination was.

She typed the address into his phone, and he followed the navigation instructions.

After a half-hour drive, they pulled into a parking lot in front of the Humane Society. A lump formed in his throat. She remembered. His *rio bonita* was taking him to get a dog—another secret longing he told her about in the drover's cabin.

When he turned off the truck, he kept his gaze forward. No woman had ever done something so special for him. And here River planned two incredible gifts just for him. If he looked at her, he might not maintain control.

He heard her suck in a sharp breath. "You're not mad, are you?"

Love expanded his chest. He turned to look at her. She bit her lower lip.

"Not in the least." He coughed. "No one has ever…"

Her teeth released her lip as she scooted closer to him. Then he reached over and cupped her cheek in his palm before he brushed his lips over hers. The fiery kiss lasted only a few seconds, but with it, he conveyed how much her surprises meant to him.

As heat warmed his cheeks, he hurried out of the truck and around to her side to help her down. Then they made their way inside the animal shelter.

"They have a lot of dogs," River said. "They are all micro-chipped and fixed. The volunteer I spoke to said we can take our time looking at the dogs and when we find one you like, you can spend some time with them to see if the dog is a good fit."

Dalton let out a shaky breath, still overwhelmed by her thoughtfulness.

"I just need to let them know we're here."

After River checked in at the front desk, they made their way down the rows of clean, climate controlled kennels. The excited yips of small dogs caused his heart to squeeze. He was finally getting a dog.

As he perused the little dogs, none drew him, so they moved to the next building with mid-sized dogs.

"Oh! Look at this sweet girl." River tried to crouch down in front of a fawn colored Staffordshire terrier. "She knows how to sit and everything."

Dalton crouched next to River. The warm-brown eyes of the staffy hooked him. Instantly. Love at first sight with a dog. Was that even possible?

Then the sweet girl's tongue lolled to the side and what he could only describe as a grin formed on the dog's face.

"You're such a sweetie, aren't you?" River asked.

Dalton helped River stand upright again. Then he scanned the information. Only a year old. The staffy had been in a home with cats and didn't get along with them. Did great with kids, men, and women. Her name was Ginger.

Dalton sniffed, almost mortified that he was getting choked up over a dog.

"You want to meet her, don't you?" River whispered.

He nodded, unable to speak.

One volunteer led them to an enclosed area where they could meet Ginger. When they led the sweet staffy toward him, he grinned. She panted and smiled. He kneeled down to let her sniff his hand, and she licked it. So he pet her back and scratched her side. She leaned into him as if to say he was her human.

"She likes you," River said, her excitement barely contained.

"I'm kinda fond of her, too."

The worker asked if River lived in the house too. She hesitated. Dalton held the gate open for her and she stepped in. Ginger sniffed the boot before she stood and placed her paws on River's thighs. River grinned from ear to ear as she rubbed the dog's head and chest.

"I'll take her," Dalton said.

River smiled at him. He would never tire of her smile.

It took another hour for them to bathe and dry Ginger, while Dalton filled out the paperwork. They sent him home with a big bag of dog food, a leash, and a few other essentials.

When he lifted the dog into the back seat, she grinned that beautiful staffy smile and he knew they would be best friends. Then he helped River into the truck.

By the time they returned to the ranch house and unpacked everything, Padre had the smoker fired up. Ginger followed Dalton around while Padre showed him how to prepare the meat. His grandfather helped with a few ribs, drawing Dalton's attention to the old man's gnarled hands. They talked and laughed as they worked. It had been a long time since he had spent this much time with Padre, and he vowed to be more intentional about it.

Padre promised to show him how to start the smoker next time. Then he told Dalton how to load it up. Ginger watched every movement with curious, warm-brown eyes. Then they sat in the air-conditioned sunroom, chatting while they occasionally checked on the meat. Ginger never left his side.

When the meat was done, his brothers arrived for the family dinner. Mami made several sides to go with the ribs. River joined them and Dalton pulled her aside.

"Thanks, River. This has been one of the best days of my life."

"You're welcome, Dalton. Looks like Padre enjoyed the day, too."

Then she stood on her tiptoes and placed a sweet kiss on his cheek before sitting in her chair at the table.

The evening continued with laughter and family stories. He fed his new dog, and he pictured many more days like this, surrounded by family, his loyal dog, and the woman he loved.

15

RIVER HAD SETTLED into a routine at the ranch. She often woke after Dalton started his day. Catalina insisted on making her breakfast most days, but today she had asked Renata to pick her up and take her to the coffee shop. She wanted time away from the house.

When Renata parked the Jeep in front of the shop, the security guard opened the passenger door for River. He retrieved her bag and crutches from the back seat before walking with her into the coffee shop. When he asked where she wanted to sit, she nodded to an empty table by the window. Then she thanked him.

Before she sat down, Drake sidled up to the table. "The usual iced mocha?"

"Yes. And a coffee cake if there's any."

"Coming right up."

She glanced up at the verse and family motto, touching her fingertips lightly against the necklace of the family brand.

What would it have been like to grow up in a family so centered on Christ? Always certain of God's presence and plan?

Far different from her own experience, she imagined. Her parents were good people and treated her well. Yet ever since she came to know Christ several years ago, she wondered if knowing Him sooner would have changed anything about her life.

She wished — no, she prayed — that one day her parents would be open to going to church with her. Her relationship with Christ had centered her. Gave her purpose. She felt His love and acceptance, even when she made poor choices. He promised never to leave her. That was what she wanted them to experience.

Lord, let the words of my novel be all that You want them to be. Let it speak into the hearts of the women who read it. May they hear the whispers of Your love for them in the pages. Please put people in Mom and Dad's life that they would come to know You. Amen.

Her phone pinged. Dalton.

Thinking of you.

Love bubbled up from her soul. She loved him even more after five weeks with him. Two more weeks before her follow up appointment with the orthopedic surgeon and she had no desire to return to Ohio. Ever.

Did Dalton want the same thing? Would he find the courage to ask her to stay?

River wasn't certain. Not after what Janessa did to him. She considered broaching the subject with him. Yet the old-fashioned part of her heart wanted him to fight for her. She would respect him more if he knew his own heart and asked her to stay, instead of the other way around.

So many questions swirled in her mind this morning. No answers. In time, they would come. She knew as she turned those worries into prayers, things would become clear in God's perfect timing.

I do not deviate from the Lord's plan.

Yes. If Dalton wanted her to stay, he would have to ask. She would let him know her feelings, but she would let him lead. Even if it meant she might have to leave with a broken heart.

A tear slid down her cheek as Drake brought her coffee cake and mocha over.

"Something wrong?" he asked.

"Just a heavy heart this morning."

He squeezed her shoulder. "Do you want me to pray with you?"

River sucked in a shaky breath. "I'll be fine. I know He hears my prayers."

Drake watched her for a few more seconds before returning to his work.

She picked up her phone and ran her thumb over Dalton's words. Then she took a selfie of her sipping her mocha and sent it to him. A few seconds later, he responded with *Mi rio bonita.*

She loved his nickname for her, and how he tied it into his mother's Mexican heritage. Out of all the Vargas boys, only Drake shared Catalina's caramel-brown coloring and black hair. Though some brothers sported dark brown hair and a nice tan, they favored their father. What had Devon called it? Oh yeah. Spanish heritage.

River ate her coffee cake before she powered on her laptop. Then she wrote in the peaceful dining hall. Words flowed in rapid succession.

After a few hours, several cowboys filtered in for a grab-and-go lunch. River smiled and greeted each of them. A few teased her, asking if her fictional cowboy hero had stacked up to them. Ego was not lacking on Vargas Ranch.

Dalton walked into the room and her breath caught at the sight of his handsome face and gold eyes. Then recognition dawned as he escorted a couple toward her.

"Look who I found," he teased.

"Mom! Dad!" she screeched as she tried to stand, knocking her booted foot against the leg of the table.

"River!"

Mom crossed the distance in an instant, swallowing her in a rejuvenating hug. She rocked River from side to side. River breathed in the familiar patchouli scent she had always associated with her. Dad waited until Mom released her before giving her a less-dramatic embrace.

"Mmm. Missed you, honey."

"What are you doing here?" she asked as she settled into the chair. She cleared her things from the table and they sat with her.

"I'll see you tonight," Dalton said after he placed a chaste kiss on her cheek. "Mamacita said to invite them for supper at the house."

She rewarded him with a soft smile. "Will do."

"We thought you could use cheering up," Dad said.

"Such lies, Ray." Mom's graying gold hair bounced as she shook her head. "Your father wanted to check out the dude ranch after all the pictures you sent."

"Guest ranch," River corrected, knowing how much the Vargases preferred the more modern name.

"We called ahead and learned there's a couple's casita open. That nice Dalton took our things over there and said you were in here."

Drake appeared at the tail end of Mom's comments. He waited for her to finish before he asked if they wanted anything.

"Oh, some chai would be lovely," Mom answered. Dad asked for a coffee with cream and sugar.

"We know there aren't as many activities in early August as there will be in September," Dad said. "But we really wanted to see you."

"How is the book?" Mom asked.

River shared the highlights. She had just started the second draft, filling in the gaps in the story. Beefing up the tension.

When their drinks were ready and Dad went to pick them up, Mom turned excited hazel eyes her way.

"Is that the necklace from Dalton?"

"Yes." River pointed to the motto over the double doors. "Their brand has dual meaning. All the firstborn sons are Dalton J. Vargas. So the lowercase 'd' and the uppercase 'V' can mean their names. When read altogether, the brand spells out 'deviate' and is a reminder of their motto."

"Oh."

Some of the brightness dimmed in Mom's eyes. She was too polite to say anything against the Bible verse. River sighed. She needed to learn to be patient.

"Are you going to stay and marry that young man?"

"He hasn't asked. So, I'm not sure. I know you and Dad still live in Ohio, but Columbus doesn't interest me any more."

"I can see why. He's quite the handsome man. And he clearly cares for you."

"I'm just trying to take it one day at a time. My foot is still healing and I'm in no rush."

"We can hardly wait to meet everyone," Dad said as he delivered their drinks.

River beamed. She knew they would come to love the Vargases as much as she did.

"What about that drone and the stalker?" Dad asked. "Have you seen any signs of him?"

"Not since my birthday. Derin hired their security guard to come back early to help watch for any signs of trouble."

She had nearly forgotten all about him. Hopefully, the stalker wouldn't show his face again.

"RIVER'S PARENTS, EH?"

Derin slapped Dalton on the shoulder, leaving his skin stinging.

"Sounds like things are getting serious."

Ginger pressed against Dalton's leg, and he leaned down to rub his hand on her head. She followed him everywhere on the ranch. She loved riding in the truck, too.

"It's not like that. They surprised her with a visit."

"Sure. And you had nothing to do with it."

When Derin grinned like a fool, Dalton held back his frown. He couldn't believe his outgoing, overconfident brother cared about love or relationships.

"Don't look like I just sprouted a second head. You love her. You're gonna marry her. It's all anyone talks about."

Great. He did not know his relationship with River fueled the ranch gossip mill. He was sure Mami would read too much into the Sloane's presence, too.

Not like he had time to linger. He had the Yavapai County chapter meeting in Prescott. After leaving Ginger in the office with Renata, he climbed behind the wheel of his truck and waved when River looked out the window. She waved back.

When he pulled onto the highway, he eased back in the seat and turned on some music. Even his favorite tunes failed to drown out Derin's earlier teasing. He wanted to beg River to stay longer—forever. As his wife.

What if her parents convinced her to go home? Would they pressure her? Would they support her if she chose him? Or would they whisk her away before he told her how he really felt about her? His mind churned over every potential obstacle standing between him and River.

An hour later, when he pulled into a parking space in Prescott, Dalton felt exhausted from the anxiety boiling in his heart. He needed to focus and prepare for the Independent Rustic Lodging Association meeting.

River had finished the website, and it went live two weeks ago. Already, several properties in the Maricopa chapter had seen increased bookings. He hoped for similar success stories today.

The second he opened the door, he knew something wasn't right. The members flashed plastic smiles his way. Not the sincere and friendly smiles he was used to.

"You have some nerve!" Ada Wilson yelled as she wagged a finger at him, one hand propped on her hip.

Dalton raised his hands. "Sorry, I don't—"

"Gage, do you have that paper?"

Gage Bishop stormed toward him and slapped a newspaper against his chest. Reflexively, Dalton's hand rested over the newsprint for a second before he turned it over to read it.

There in living color were pictures of him and River. Not only from the Independence Day celebration. Also pictures from a recent dinner in town—one where he had stolen a passionate kiss from her before closing his truck door. The picture from the drover's cabin was the most damning. The angle made it look like they were on the brink of making love. Nothing could be further from the truth.

The air whooshed from his lungs. His throat constricted.

Impossible. How could there be any pictures from the drover's cabin?

"You manipulated us into paying your lover to build a website for us!" Ada accused.

"She's not—"

"We thought you had morals!" Beatrice Mason said. "That. That. Picture." Fierce brown eyes revealed her utter disdain.

"It's not like that. River is my girlfriend, but we never—"

"Sure looks like you did," Gage groused.

"We voted to remove you from the chapter," Ada announced. "We only want to deal with reputable businessmen and you, sir, are not that!"

Dalton clamped his jaw tight. His eyes scanned the faces in the room. Anger and disappointment greeted him.

"It was a unanimous decision," Beatrice added.

He clenched the newspaper in his fisted hand and stormed from the building. Once in the solitude of his truck, he slammed his palm against the steering wheel. Then he wiped a hand over his face.

He glanced at the pictures, heart sinking through the

floorboard of his truck. Had River seen these? Had her parents?

How did they have pictures from the cabin? The door had been closed. It had been raining. No drone would have been able to fly through that downpour.

Dalton's heart hammered as he drove home.

The locked door in the drover's cabin.

Why had someone locked the door in the drover's cabin? Who locked it?

It made no sense. No one in his family would have done it. They had other similar structures on the property and they had no locks just in case someone ended up stranded, like he and River had.

Dalton asked his phone to dial Derin.

"D4. What's up?"

"Take the security guard and head out to the drover's cabin."

"The drover's cabin?"

"Yeah. Something isn't right. I'm staring at pictures of me and River that could have only come from inside that cabin. On the day we sheltered there."

A low whistle came across the line. "You don't think the drone creep has been hiding out there, do you? Maybe he was the one who cut the fence."

"It's the only thing that makes sense."

"We'll check out all the outbuildings."

"I'll be home around dinner. Let's talk then."

Dalton ended the call.

The last thing he wanted to do was show River the pictures. But he knew he had to. She needed to know about it.

Lord, please help us catch this guy. Keep River safe. Help me find the words to ease her fears.

He dialed his father next and asked him to gather his brothers for a meeting in his office. They needed to sort this out immediately.

16

_____

"RIO BONITA!" CATALINA greeted her with a warm hug. "This must be your mami and papi."

River smiled and introduced Dalton's mom to her parents. As Catalina peppered them with several questions, River looked around the room. No Dalton. No Ginger with her staffy grin and wagging whip tail.

"Let me take you on a tour," Catalina said as she directed her parents toward the kitchen.

River tuned her ear for any sound. Muffled voices came from Dalton's office, so she balanced her crutches under her arms and headed that way. She paused just outside the door.

"...she safe?"

"...found more photos. Locked door."

Her heart pounded against her chest. What photos? She slowly turned the knob and eased the door open.

"How many photos?" Dalton asked. He stood staring out the window with tightly fisted hands at his side. When Ginger pressed against his leg, his hands relaxed and he crouched down to scratch behind her ears.

"Hundreds."

He whirled around, brow furrowed and fierce eyes flaming. When his gaze snagged on her, she swallowed the lump in her throat. Ginger noticed her and bounded over, tail wagging and tongue lolling.

"What's going on?" she asked. Pressure started behind

her eyes and wrapped around her temples.

Every Vargas male swiveled to face her. Dalton's jaw twitched as he softened his expression, crossing the room. She caught a whiff of his cologne as he helped her ease into a chair. The normally comforting scent failed to calm her.

"Dalton?"

Her neck and shoulders tensed as she studied their grim expressions. Dalton sucked in a deep breath and released it in a rush.

"There are pictures of us in the tabloids."

"What?!" Her shrill voice cut through the silence.

She started to rise, but Dalton rested a hand on her shoulder. Then he crouched in front of her. He clasped her icy hands in his warm ones. Ginger whined from her spot next to him.

"The pictures paint an unflattering story of us."

"Can I see them?"

Dalton glanced away.

Derin cleared his throat. "I don't think it's a good idea."

River narrowed her eyes and straightened in her chair. "Now I definitely want to see them. I need to know what's circulating about me."

Dalton held out his hand. Derin slapped a newspaper in it before Dalton handed it to her.

"I... Came across this today."

River stared at the tabloid, trying to make sense of the photos. Dalton and her in the hot tub the night he told her about the barbed wire scar. A special moment between them. Invaded and made public.

Her eyes burned as they shifted to the next picture. Dalton's amazing kiss in the truck after they left the restaurant last week. It was their only official date away from the Vargas property. They had gone because they felt safe.

Her hands shook and a heart-wrenching groan wrested from her throat. Dalton holding her close in the drover's cabin. Kissing her. The angle made it look like she straddled him.

"How?" A sob caught in her throat. Her eyes flicked to his. "How could they have this?" Her finger poked the picture from the cabin.

Dalton's mouth turned down. The pictures hurt him. She could see it in his gaze. Ginger pushed her head under his hand, offering her furry comfort.

"Someone had been living in the locked room in the drover's cabin. Derin found a hidden camera in the room we were in."

"Do they have audio? Do they know what we..."

She choked on the question. The secrets they had both shared. That was private. Only for Dalton's ears. Not the public.

Derin answered, "As best we can tell, it only recorded video. No audio."

"Was there someone there when we were?" Her throat constricted over the possibility and her headache pounded.

Dalton shook his head. "There was only one way in and out. The lock only worked from the outside of the door."

River's hands shook. "What else?"

"There were pictures from the fourth, but not the one your stalker sent."

Her heart throbbed so hard she thought it might fly out of her chest.

"What are you saying?"

"The sheriff's deputy is dusting for prints," Derin said. "But he thinks there were multiple people watching you."

River felt light-headed. Her vision narrowed, and she flopped her back against the seat. She closed her eyes. Ginger leaned against her leg and River patted her head. This could not be happening to her. She was a romance writer. Nobody. Okay, so she had a few bestsellers, but who cared? Who would want to stalk her, much less publicize something in a tabloid about her?

"Give us a minute." Dalton's voice sounded far away.

Tears streamed down her cheeks. How much had they documented about their relationship? What did these people plan to do with the other pictures? Could she and Dalton go anywhere without being recognized? What did this mean to her career?

"River. Breathe."

The touch of his fingers curling around hers caused her eyes to snap open, and she stared up into his face.

"We'll get through this. I promise. We'll find these jerks."

So they hadn't found them. Just the evidence they had been there. Invading every sacred moment. She felt violated and exposed.

She blinked and straightened her back as she withdrew her hand from his. "I'm sorry. I'm sorry I brought this trouble to your doorstep."

Her heart cracked into a thousand shards. She knew what she had to do. She had to leave. Leave Dalton. Go back to Ohio.

A sob choked her. She couldn't leave him. She loved him.

"River." Dalton's voice filled with concern. "Don't pull away from me."

She shook her head. "I need…"

River reached for her crutches and pushed up from the chair. Dalton stood in her way.

"Move." Her voice cracked under the weight of her breaking heart.

"Don't do this. Please. I love you. We can face this together."

She swallowed down the boulder in her throat, refusing to make eye contact with him.

"Please move," she whispered.

With an exasperated sigh, he stepped aside.

Each *click thump* of her crutches felt like another wound ripping open in her soul. She had to get out of there. It was the only option. This negative publicity could destroy every-thing the Vargases had built—Dalton had built.

It was all her fault. She had brought danger to their doorstep. In the end, she had been worse for him than Janessa. And she would never forgive herself for it.

DALTON RAN A hand through his hair. He knew the mo-ment he lost her. He saw it in the straightening of her back. The light in his *rio bonita*'s eyes disappeared, replaced with a heart-breaking dullness. She was going to leave.

His stomach clenched hard, along with his heart and his soul. He couldn't lose her. And he couldn't go after her. Not then. She needed time.

Lord, this can't be Your plan. I don't accept it. I was certain You brought us together. How can You let this happen? How can You tear her away from me?

He sat staring at the doorway where River had left. Numbness spread through his heart and limbs. What could he say or do to convince her to stay? Had he lost her forever?

Ginger curled up by his feet, a small comfort in his heartache.

"Son."

Dalton stirred at the sound of Papi's voice.

"They're gone."

He nodded solemnly. He had already felt his heart de-parting.

"They're flying back tomorrow."

Dalton bowed his head and pinched the bridge of his nose.

"River wouldn't listen to reason," Papi said. "Not from me or Catalina. Nor her parents."

"I." Dalton coughed. "I know."

"You hungry?"

He shook his head. Nothing would ever be the same again. Not without her smile. Not without her humor or laughter. Nor her gentle touch or her soul-stirring presence.

Papi offered a sympathetic smile before swinging the door shut with a soft click.

Good. Dalton couldn't stomach food. Or words. Or family. Or anything.

He picked up his phone and tapped on his text message app. His thumb hovered over River's name. He tapped on it. The picture of her in the dining hall sipping a mocha — the last message she had sent him.

Longing greater than he could handle flooded his soul. He didn't want to let her go without a fight. Yet she wouldn't listen. He had learned enough about her to know it.

Please don't give up on us, rio bonita. Give me a chance. I'll walk through fire for you. I'll never leave you, if you would only let me.

The words collided with his heart. Wasn't that what God promised him? God would never leave him alone.

What do I do, Lord?

His phone light dimmed, then faded to black. Ginger rested her head on his feet, letting him know she was here for him.

If you love her, let her go.

No! He didn't want to let her go. How could that be God's answer? How could it be His plan?

His stomach churned. His pride burned. He wanted things to unfold in his timing, not God's. He wanted his way, not God's. With River, Dalton wanted to control the outcome and the timing.

Not my will, but Yours. The simple prayer begrudgingly tore from his soul.

The tiny seeds of peace buried deep in his heart. Perhaps God had a bigger plan — one that required Dalton J. Vargas the fourth, to trust Him in everything and with everything, including River.

Pray. He had to surrender his will. His timing.

Dalton shoved back his chair and dropped to his knees, resting his forearms on his desk. Ginger shifted to rest her back against his leg, while he prayed like he had never prayed before. He prayed for River. That God would heal her pain. That God would speak to her heart. Give her wisdom. He prayed for her novel. That it would be an enormous success and the message — what had she said it was? That's right, God's timing. He prayed the message would resonate with those who read it.

God's timing.

Hope rebuilt his broken heart. They weren't over and done. River wasn't lost to him forever. No. He knew it. This time apart was for her sake. Some work God needed to do in her heart.

Perhaps it was for him as well.

Dalton realized he had never truly forgiven Janessa. Never admitted his own wrongs in that relationship. His pride prevented him from seeing the chip on his shoulder as large as Dalton Peak. He had been wrong to blame everything on Janessa. Dalton repented.

His heart gushed with regret over thinking the success or failure of the ranch rested solely on his shoulders. He was only a steward of Vargas Ranch. Of the resort. Just like Mami said, if God blessed it or ended it, God's plan for the ranch was what would happen. Not Dalton's plan. Or Derin's. Or Papi's or Padre's.

Stewards. Caretakers.

Lord, I'm sorry I never asked what You want this place to be. I've not approached it with a humble attitude. Forgive me. Show me what You desire Vargas Guest Ranch & Resort to be. Even if it's something a little different for each soul that crosses the dining hall threshold.

Ideas sprang to his mind. He pushed up from the floor and settled into his office chair. Punching the power button on his laptop, he waited for it to boot up. Then he typed out a business plan for the next three years. The new programs they needed to offer—especially for children. Who they needed to hire. The financing required. How he could enlist his brothers to take on a more active role in the areas that interested them.

And all for God's glory. Not the Vargas name. Not Dalton's name.

When he finished well after midnight, he printed out seven copies of the plan and set them on the corner of his desk. He would share it with his father, brothers, and Renata soon.

He padded to the back door and let Ginger into the backyard, breathing deeply of the warm night air while she took care of business. When she bounded over to him, he held the door open. Then he walked down the hall to his bedroom, Ginger's nails clicking on the tile behind him. She curled up in her fluffy round bed, her soft snores brought a smile to his face.

As he climbed into bed, his last thoughts were: *We do not deviate from the Lord's plan.*

Peace filled his heart. All would be exactly as God intended it to be and in His perfect timing.

17

RIVER TOSSED AND turned all night long on the sleeper sofa in the great room of her parents' rented casita — the same one she had stayed in. The one where Dalton smiled at her from the doorway before he shut off the water to the kitchenette sink.

Nothing felt right. She hated that her fame brought trouble to the Vargas family and especially to Dalton. If the stalker or paparazzi intended damage to her or the Vargases, she had one choice. Go home.

Except Ohio wasn't home anymore. Vargas Guest Ranch & Resort was.

No, that wasn't true. Her home had become a person. One sexy, golden-eyed cowboy who had lassoed her heart without even tossing a rope in her direction.

She loved him. Everything about him. His demeanor. His character. He exhibited leadership. His faith was strong. Dalton was everything she wanted in a man.

But she couldn't let her desire to be with him bring more trouble to his doorstep or his family. As much as it pained her, she needed to go back to Ohio. Wrap up her novel. Take the danger away before it destroyed the man she loved.

Tears streamed down her cheeks. She had always thought the plot twist towards the end of a novel never happened in real life. It was meant to hook the reader through the end of the book. The hero and heroine were torn apart.

Will they get back together or not?

It had worked on her, causing her to lose sleep reading to the end of many romance novels.

She just never expected it to happen in her life. Not with Dalton.

The kitchenette light flipped on. River groaned and tossed aside the throw blanket covering her legs.

"What time is our flight?" she asked her dad.

"We don't have to go, honey."

"Dad—"

"You can stay. Marry your cowboy, paparazzi be hanged."

"It's not that simple. They still haven't caught the stalker either."

Her dad held her gaze for several seconds. He had always read her. A frown flitted across his face.

"What time?" she asked again.

"Nine. We need to leave in an hour."

She nodded and removed the boot. Then she showered and dressed for the most heartbreaking day of her life. The day she would say goodbye to Dalton. If she even saw him.

By the time Dad packed the rental car, River had seen no sign of the Vargases. Solana manned the office alone and checked them out. Heart heavy, River slid into the back seat of the rental car.

The desert drive seemed prettier this time. Dalton Peak glowed in the early morning sun. Golden rays cast red and purple shadows over its craggy face. The green palo verde trees waved goodbye to her in a gentle breeze, their yellow flowers long gone. The tall, fat saguaro cacti stood sentry as Dad pulled onto the paved highway. Bright blue sky, more luminous than the sky in Ohio, domed over them.

She would miss Arizona too.

At the airport gate, she glanced around the terminal one last time, uncertain what she expected to see. People sat in seats. A baby cried and her mother tried to comfort her. A young man's foot bobbed up and down as his thumbs flew across the screen of his phone.

A man walked away from her in dark jeans. Dark brown cowboy boots and a nicely tailored jacket. No aviator sunglasses. Not that she could tell. He reminded her of Dalton. The man didn't look at her.

She let out a soft sigh as the flight attendant allowed passengers needing assistance—her with her bulky boot and crutches—to board. Her parents boarded with her.

When the plane taxied from the gate, any hope of a romantic airport reunion with Dalton faded into an unfulfilled fantasy. She hadn't expected it. Real life and all.

It would make a brilliant scene in a novel. Maybe in her second cowboy romance, she would work it in.

The plane sped down the tarmac and into the air with that feeling of three seconds of weightlessness that never failed to make her feel slightly woozy. The sensation faded, and she rested her head against the seat back. In a few hours, she would land back home. All hope of seeing Dalton again diminished.

RIVER'S PARENTS KINDLY drove her back to her apartment and helped her with her luggage. The crutches made travel more difficult, and she appreciated they went an hour out of their way to help her. She would have to find an orthopedic surgeon. See if she couldn't ditch the boot soon.

After they left, she ordered beef lo mein. While she waited, she unpacked and started a load of laundry. Then she set her laptop on the kitchen bar and turned it on.

Her phone pinged, alerting her that her food had arrived. She hopped over to the door on one crutch and retrieved the meal. Then she sat at the bar and slurped her favorite noodles.

River opened her novel. Moisture gathered in the corners of her eyes. It should have felt good to be home. Except it didn't. She missed her real cowboy. Her love. Her Dalton. She wiped her eyes on the rough napkin from the Chinese food place.

A new scene came to mind. She found the spot for it in her manuscript. Then she closed her eyes and allowed the words to flow through her fingers onto the screen. All the pain River felt in that moment — the homesickness for Dalton — formed into a dramatic, heart-wrenching scene, pushing her characters to the end of themselves.

Her eyes flew open. Her heart squeezed tight. Not once during the last few days had she prayed.

Lord, what is wrong with me? How could I forget to seek You in all of this?

Silence filled her apartment. She waited, fingertips resting above the keys.

God's timing. The theme of her novel. The theme of her current circumstances.

Words gushed from her soul, and her fingers frantically flew over the keys. God wanted her heart. He wanted her obedience. Releasing her will and her plans.

We do not deviate from the Lord's plan.

What was the verse on the dining hall's wall? River snatched her phone. Had she taken a picture of it?

She flipped through picture after picture from Vargas Ranch. Dalton. Dalton. Dalton. His family. The beautiful desert. A desert, bleak and barren one moment and so full of life in the next. Dalton. Drake. Derin being silly. She snorted.

There! The verse.

With regard to the works of man, by the word of your lips I have avoided the ways of the violent. My steps have held fast to your paths; my feet have not slipped. Psalms 17:4-5.

Her breath caught in her throat. By God's word. Avoided the ways of the violent.

She had made a terrible mistake. Huge.

The verse told her exactly what to do to avoid the ways of the violent. Rely on God's Word. Hold fast to His path. She hadn't done that. Instead, she ran as fast and hard as she could.

God was sovereign. More powerful than any stalker or paparazzi. He could do all things. He spoke the world into existence.

What had she said to the Vargases that first night in the dining hall? That she believed God's Word was a guide for life.

Yet when faced with a fearful circumstance, she had completely neglected Him and His Word. She had run. She ran toward the familiar and her own wisdom. Not the wisdom of those who cared for her. The Vargases and her parents warned her to stay. To walk beside Dalton through this mess.

No, she had run like the fool she was.

A sob escaped her throat. Sorrow overwhelmed her. Words wrenched from her soul.

Lord. I'm so sorry. When it mattered the most, I didn't live like I believed You, like I trusted You. Forgive me. Help me make this right.

After several minutes praying, River finally opened her eyes. The last words she had written flashed on the screen.

"Not in my timing, but in God's."

The words wrapped around her heart like a father's loving embrace. All was not lost. In God's timing, she would find her way home.

18

"THIS LOOKS AMAZING," Papi said. "I would have never thought of half of these things."

"Love the sports complex idea," Derin said. "With the tennis court already under construction on that side of the property, we've got more land to build around it."

"Would you manage it?" Dalton asked, pleased at the excitement lighting his brother's eyes.

"Ah. I don't know. I'm just a cowboy."

Devon snorted. "Just? Are you kidding?"

"Yeah," Drake added. "You're a leader. The men hang on your every word. You could totally do this."

Dalton rubbed Ginger's head as he studied Derin. His brother rubbed a hand over his face. Then he locked onto Dalton.

"Do you really think I could do something like that? I'm not a businessperson. Not trained like you are."

"You can learn what you need to," Dalton said, moving to stand next to his brother. He rested a hand on his shoulder and squeezed. "You've got a lot of natural talent. I'll help you."

"I don't know. You'll be pretty busy, from the looks of it." Derin swept his hand over the business plan.

Dalton laughed. "I'm not doing all of this."

He shifted and looked each of his brothers in the eye. "You are."

"We are?" Dylan squeaked.

"Dylan, you'll take over everything with the horses. The stables. Trail ride plans. Purchasing, training, grooming. There's room in the budget for you to hire more staff to help, but you need to run it."

Dylan's eyes widened.

"Mijo, you can do this." Mami squeezed Dylan's hand. "It's horses and you love horses."

"Renata, you and Solana are going to expand the spa. If one of you wants to manage it, then I'm all for it. If not, then we will hire a manager."

"I'll pray about it," Renata said.

Best answer he had heard yet.

"Devon." He waited for his brother's full attention. "I want you to lead the children's program or manage who does. You love teaching kids, so come up with a plan for educational activities. Fun activities. If you have ideas that require construction or investments, let me know. I'm here to support you. But you can dream big on this."

Devon beamed, answer enough.

"Drake."

He turned to the youngest Vargas brother. Still so much to learn at twenty-one. Dalton knew his plan would require Drake to step up. Same plan, different approach.

"You'll apprentice with Renata for a year in preparation to take over all operations for the dining hall, coffee shop, catering, and whatever else we need. If you have ideas, bring them to the team. If you feel overwhelmed, speak up. I'll help too."

Drake nodded slowly.

"When the time is right, we can hire more seasonal and permanent staff. You'll be part of those decisions. It won't be me and Renata deciding for you."

"Understood."

Then Dalton turned toward his parents. "Mami. Papi."

Mami smiled softly. Papi's eyes narrowed.

"I need you to manage the grounds. Help as you see fit and hire for what you don't want to do. And Papi?"

"Son?"

"I'll need your help to hire or promote a foreman for the ranch, since Derin's focus is changing."

"Done."

"Thank you. And thank you all for believing in me and this plan."

Padre cleared his throat. "Let's pray over this."

They all rose to their feet and stood in a circle, hands clasped.

Padre's voice sounded gravelly at first. It cleared as his prayer continued.

"Lord, we ask for your blessing on these bold new plans. Let Vargas Guest Ranch & Resort be a place where hurting hearts come for healing and rest. Let them encounter you in these programs. Let them find the peace that only You bring. Give us the energy to accomplish this impressive feat. Give Dalton continued wisdom to listen to Your voice and guidance. Help us make this place all that You want it to be."

"And bring River home," Mami added.

Ginger barked and wagged her tail at the mention of River's name. She missed his *rio bonita* as much as he did.

Goosebumps pricked Dalton's skin as he joined his family, reciting their mission statement. "We do not deviate from the Lord's plan. Amen."

With God on their side, and a surrendered heart in him, Dalton prayed their plans would help many people for generations to come.

Renata excused herself, not wanting to leave Solana alone for too long.

Papi followed Mami into the kitchen and began setting out a sizable feast as Dalton cleared the papers from the table.

Derin pulled him aside and asked several questions about the sports complex. He made a few suggestions, too.

Like connecting with his sports agent friend. He wanted to advertise Vargas Guest Ranch & Resort as a place where athletes could recover from injuries. A team of sports medicine professionals on staff during peak season. Dalton loved the ideas. They would iron out the details and timing later.

Devon chatted with Mami during the meal and tossed out ideas for children's activities. He even jotted down some notes on the back of the business plan. For once, Mami didn't squash the business conversation at the dinner table.

As he looked at the enthusiastic faces around him, pride welled in Dalton's chest. They all embraced his ideas and brought many of their own. This was a turning point for their family business.

And the only thing missing was River.

His attention dropped to his plate, and he picked up a grilled chicken street taco, after dousing it with a few drops of sriracha. As he swallowed a bite, Papi leaned over.

"When are you gonna bring your woman back here?"

Dalton frowned. He had felt God telling him to let her go.

"She belongs at your side."

"I haven't heard from her since she left."

Not a call or a text in two weeks. His heart ached as if sliced through with a knife. He missed her.

How many times had his eyes drifted toward the drover's cabin? Memories of her drenched braid. Her fear-filled eyes. She had trusted him—a flawed ranch manager—to save her.

Her unwavering belief in him. Her laughter when he told her the name of his mountain. He loved her. She would become his wife. He knew it.

"In God's timing," he whispered.

"Son, have you asked when that is?"

Dalton blinked. "No."

"Maybe you should."

OUT OF THAT dreaded boot at last! River wanted to dance down the hallway of the doctor's office, but the orthopedic surgeon warned her to take it easy for a while. She needed physical therapy for a few weeks before he would clear her for normal activity. He also said there was no lasting ligament damage. Thank goodness.

When her phone rang, Kendra's name popped on the screen.

"River. I love it! The editors love it!"

"Really?"

"Yes. They have a few suggestions they'll send over soon. And the title—*Her Hero Cowboy*—perfect!"

River smiled as Kendra continued.

"Tell me you have book two started."

"It's about fifty percent complete."

"Amazing! Looking forward to reading it. And book three."

After River hung up, she sent a prayer heavenward. *Thank you, Lord, for giving me the words to write and for Kendra's enthusiastic response.*

As she reached her car in the parking lot, she glanced up at the rain-laden clouds overhead. So different from the monsoon storm in Arizona. The sky had sparkled bright blue with puffy white clouds one minute. The next minute, dust, rain, thunder, and lightning had rolled in from nowhere.

She missed Dalton, and the gray skies cried for her.

River shook off her gloom and drove to the grocery store. After parking, she darted into the store, hoping the drizzle wouldn't turn into a downpour. A twenty-something man with light brown hair offered her a cart before stepping around her for another one.

"You!" Her breath left in a rush.

"Oh. Miss Sloane. Sorry, I didn't realize it was you."

River dug around in her purse. Where was her phone?

"You probably think I'm a creepy stalker dude."

"Um. Yeah." Her eyes went wide. Phone. She needed to call the police.

"I'm not."

"Pardon me if I don't take your word for it," she said as her fingers finally curled around her phone.

"I suppose the whole Arizona thing could appear that way."

River growled. "You sent me this picture."

She flipped to it and flashed the photo in his face.

"Not one of my finer moments. This frightening old cowboy threatened to slash my tires if I didn't send that picture to you."

"You expect me to believe that?!"

The young man's face twisted. "I guess not. Let me explain."

River's thumb hovered over 911 as a crowd gathered around them. She would give him about thirty more seconds to clear up the matter. If it could be cleared up.

Her stalker's shoulders slumped. "This all started out innocently enough. You see, my fiancée is a huge fan of yours."

Fiancée? Her brows drew together.

"She really wants you to offer a toast at our wedding."

As she sputtered, he held up his hands.

"I know. Crazy, right?" The next words he muttered. "Guess not as crazy as flying to Arizona to ask and then not do it."

River took a step back.

"I'm sorry to have scared you, Miss Sloane. It was all an act of love for Olivia. One that sounded good in my head and kinda went haywire in the attempt. Anyway, I'll be going now. Sorry again."

"You aren't going anywhere. Not after spying on me

with that drone. And the other pictures—"

"What other pictures? What drone? I don't have a drone. Don't know how to fly one."

River's blood boiled, and her face heated.

The young man's face blanched. "The creepy cowboy. He was taking pictures of you?"

"What cowboy?"

The young man flipped through pictures on his phone. Then he showed River a man she had never seen before.

"He's the one that asked me to send that picture to you. He's the one that gave me your number."

Nothing made sense. River's stomach roiled. The stalker wasn't a stalker after all. Just a love struck lunatic. Okay, maybe "lunatic" was a bit much.

"Can you send me that?" she asked.

"Are you sure?"

She growled and stepped closer, wagging a finger in his face. "You really messed up, buddy. Unless you want to take the fall for that man's invasion of privacy, you better send me that picture."

"Okay, okay."

The young man tapped on his phone a few times. Then River's chimed with the new picture.

"What was your name, again?" she asked.

"Calvin. I'm so sorry, Miss Sloane. I really just wanted to surprise Olivia. I know it was stupid."

As he turned to go, she saw the sincerity in his face. All those times she ran into him around town...

"Had you tried to ask me before? Around town?"

"Yeah, like a dozen times. Oh. I. Sorry. I guess that was pretty stalkerish, huh?"

River nodded, barely holding back a sardonic retort.

"Can you call her?" She needed to be sure this Olivia really existed and if Calvin's story was true.

"Sure." He punched his fiancée's contact and put it on speakerphone. "Hey, honey bunny. You'll never guess who

I'm standing next to."

"Who?" A soft, feminine voice came across the speaker.

"River Sloane."

The young woman's squeal hurt River's ears.

"Put her on video. Oh, please, please, please."

Calvin raised an eyebrow, and River nodded. Then he pointed the phone at her.

"Hi, Olivia," River said.

"Oh, my gosh. Oh, my gosh. Oh, my gosh!"

"Calvin said you're getting married soon."

Olivia fanned her somewhat pale face. "Yeah. In October."

"You want to have the wedding in Arizona?" River asked, thinking she had to be certifiably insane to actually agree to the couple's wish.

"Why?"

"Cause that's where I'll be in October." And for every day of the rest of her life.

Olivia and Calvin started a conversation. River backed away. They had her number. If they decided on her terms, she would toast them. As long as they allowed her a plus one.

In the meantime, she had some stuff to pack and a plane ticket to buy. After she called a sheriff's deputy in Arizona.

19

DALTON'S HEART HAMMERED in his chest. The sheriff deputy's message left him uneasy. He had an update on the stalker and the person who took the pictures. He asked Dalton to drive into Wickenburg and meet at the station there.

Dalton sighed. August had turned to September. By now, River had to be out of that awful boot. Or she might have had surgery. Yikes. He hoped not.

Either way, he had heard nothing from her.

Not a day went by he didn't think about her. Every morning, he prayed for her. Every evening, too. He thought about texting her a dozen times, but always held back. It didn't feel like God's timing. Not yet. Maybe soon? He hoped so.

The ranch had been a flurry of activity getting ready for their first guests arriving in September. Like every year, they stressed about the start of the season. Everything fell into place at the last minute. Minor tweaks here and there resolved any issues before guests became aware.

The only thing missing was River. The thought plagued him every day. She belonged at the ranch. In the ranch house. In his arms. As his wife.

If he could fly to Ohio today, he would. Ring in hand. Beg her to come home.

It would be tough to squeeze a trip in, but his family would support him. Something he should have always known, but had never asked for. Now that he had asked for their help to manage things, he would never doubt it again.

As Dalton pulled his truck into a spot outside of the Wickenburg sheriff's office, a woman with long blond hair ducked into the building. The blue sundress she wore reminded him of River. Only it couldn't be her. She was in Ohio. On the other side of the country. A dull ache spread across his chest, and he rubbed a hand over it.

He let out a slow breath before turning off his truck. Then he headed into the building. He squinted in the dim light until he took off his aviator sunglasses, tucking them into his shirt pocket.

"I'm looking for Deputy Gomez," he said as he approached the reception desk.

"Down the hall. Last door on the right."

Dalton thanked the young woman before he ambled down the hall, boots clomping on the tile. When he neared, he saw the blue sundress and blond-haired woman. His throat went dry. Her gait reminded him of River, the sway of her hips and shapely calfs. Maybe he missed her so much, he only thought he saw her everywhere he went.

When the deputy waved him in, the woman glanced over her shoulder. Dalton's feet stopped. His hand gripped the doorknob. He nearly stopped breathing.

"River."

Her hazel eyes sparkled at him as a smile stretched across her luscious pink lips. His breath caught in his throat as she whispered his name. His eyes drank her in like cold water on a hot Arizona day.

In half a second, he swept her into his arms and planted a hard kiss against her lips. She melted against him, hands sliding up his chest, resting behind his neck. He wanted to go on kissing her, but he needed to see her eyes. Her face. Her smile.

Dalton ended the kiss and held her slightly away from him. Yeah, he had just kissed the right woman. His *rio bonita*.

She released a breathy laugh. "Nice greeting, cowboy. Just don't greet Deputy Gomez that way. Don't think he'd like it."

Dalton roared as heat warmed his face and neck. He placed his hand on the small of her back and led her to a chair. Then he held out his hand to the deputy for a shake.

"Mr. Vargas. As I mentioned on the phone, I have an update on the drone case."

Dalton laced his fingers with River's. He glanced over. She was really there. In the flesh. At his side. He wished he could take her straight to the ranch to catch up.

Instead, he forced his attention back onto the deputy.

"The stalker ended up not being a threat," Deputy Gomez said.

Dalton raised an eyebrow.

River giggled. "It's a long, but romantic story. Let's just say he was never a threat. Just a hopeless romantic trying to give his fiancée the surprise of her life."

That explained nothing, but he would wait for the long story from her beautiful lips later.

"The drone operator," Deputy Gomez said. "Is in serious trouble."

"You found him?" Dalton asked, straightening in his chair.

"I think you know him. Howard Pollard."

Dalton coughed. "Howard? But why?"

"It had nothing to do with me," River explained. "And everything to do with your grandfather."

"Padre? How? Why?"

As his chest tightened, River nodded.

"Howard planned to harm your business financially," Deputy Gomez said. "More than just getting you kicked out of the Independent Rustic Lodging Association."

Dalton's heart sped up. He dropped his hold on River's hand and rubbed his hands on the arms of the chair. "Why?"

"Seems Howard has been looking for an opportunity to

get back at Dalton J. Vargas, Jr., for decades."

"Padre?"

"Yes," River said. "It's about Elena."

"My grandmother?"

Nothing they said made any sense. He took a deep breath. "Tell me everything."

"Turns out," River said, "That Howard was in love with Elena. He planned to marry her. Was all set with a wedding date and everything."

Deputy Gomez's eyes glinted as he took over telling the story. "Weeks before the wedding, she met your grandfather. Rumor has it she fell for him instantly."

"But I thought Padre said she had been a guest at the ranch."

"She and her family were. They lived in Prescott and came down for a few weeks in the winter to finish planning her wedding. To Howard!" River's voice squealed. "Can you believe it? Padre stole Howard's fiancée!"

Dalton shook his head. "And let me guess, Howard never forgave him."

"Exactly," Deputy Gomez interjected. "He's been looking for an opportunity to get back at him for decades. When Miss Sloane, a somewhat famous romance author, came to town, it provided the perfect solution for his revenge. Or so he thought."

"How did you figure all this out?"

River replied, "Well, I ran into my not-really-a-stalker stalker back in Ohio. In the grocery store. He confessed he really just wanted to ask me to offer a toast at his wedding because his fiancée is a huge fan. During that conversation, he told me that Howard asked him to send a picture to my phone. He had been frightened, so he did it."

Dalton rubbed a hand over his face. Bizarre.

God's timing.

The words echoed in his mind. Long after the rest of the conversation with the deputy.

In the end, the deputy could only charge Howard with trespassing and harassment. Dalton decided not to press charges. No point in fueling the decades old grudge. Howard had to be in his late seventies, like Padre. It didn't seem right to prosecute a flimsy case against a misguided, heartbroken old man.

"So, cowboy," River said outside of the sheriff's office. "Can you give me a lift?"

"Where to?"

"Home to Vargas Ranch."

His heart soared.

RIVER STAYED WITH Renata in the women's housing on the ranch. September gave way to early October, bringing cooler temperatures in the low nineties. Hot but not so hot. She loved Arizona, she thought as she donned a pair of bootcut jeans and a yellow snap front shirt. She threaded her new brown belt through the loops and fastened the sparkly big belt buckle together. The ivory cowboy hat completed the look. She even felt like a real cowgirl in the getup.

"Where are you going again?" Renata asked.

"A picnic at the base of Dalton Peak."

"Sounds nice. It'll be cool for several hours yet. Have fun!"

Then Renata held the door open. River followed her out. Renata waved before she whipped her Jeep out of her parking spot.

River giggled as she climbed into her brand new truck. Much to her boyfriend's dismay, it was a Toyota Tacoma and not a Ford. A girl couldn't change everything for her man. She turned the key, and it turned over with that thrilling guttural growl. She loved that sound—a reminder of how much she belonged at Vargas Ranch.

When she pulled up to the stables, Dalton had two horses saddled. Drat. She kinda liked it when he let her groom and saddle her own.

He opened her truck door and held out his hand for her. She accepted it even though she normally just slid out of her truck. Once her feet rested on the ground, Dalton closed the door and pulled her into his arms. His lips brushed quickly across hers, stealing her breath away.

"Ready?"

She nodded, still trying to catch her breath. Then he gave her a leg up. Once settled on Sunflower's back, she nudged the mare into a gentle lope. Dalton rode up next to her.

A snicker bubbled up. "I'm surprised you'd take me on a picnic."

"Why's that?"

"You remember the last one?"

Dalton beamed. "I enjoyed it so much. I don't know if we'll top that one."

River laughed. "If you want to carry me on your back, I'm game."

"I could do without the rain. And monsoon season is over. I think we're safe."

"Oh, well. I thought you looked pretty good in the drover's cabin."

He shook his head, laughing.

"Race you," Dalton said before he kicked Toasted Toffee into a canter. River matched his pace until he slowed. She placed a hand on top of her hat and let out a hearty chuckle.

"That was fun!"

"Do you know who named Dalton Peak?" he asked as he reined in his horse.

"No, I don't."

She dismounted, and he took her reins, tying both horses to a low mesquite tree.

"My great-grandmother."

"There's more to this story, isn't there?" she asked as Dalton clasped her hand and led them several feet away.

"Yes. A few years before they moved here, they explored the area, looking for the best place for a dude ranch. She brought great-grandpa to this spot—"

He took several exaggerated steps.

"Here."

Then he faced her, dropping to one knee. River's breath left in a rush as she rested her hand on her chest.

"*Mi rio bonita*, in this place that is special to my family, I have one very important question for you."

She smiled.

"Hungry?"

When his face split into a grin, she laughed. "Famished."

"Good. But that wasn't my question."

"No. I don't think it was."

"River Sloane, will you marry me? Be my wife? Live on this ranch, our home, for the rest of our lives?"

She threw her arms around his neck, tumbling them both to the ground. "Yes! Yes! Yes!"

Then her real cowboy captured her lips with his, sealing a promise that would last a lifetime.

Epilogue

DYLAN STOOD NEXT to his older brother, pride nearly busting his fancy shirt buttons apart. They stood at the front of the cowboy church as soft music played. When River appeared at the back, hand resting lightly on Ray Sloane's arm, Dylan shot a glance at his older brother.

Yeah, Dalton loved that woman with his entire being. Dylan understood it. Had felt the same way about one very special woman ever since high school. At least Dalton's dream came true.

As Dalton and River exchanged vows, Dylan's mind wandered to his one true love. Too bad he would never have his happily ever after. Women weren't the only ones that desired such things. He did. He wanted to marry her. Have children with her.

Stupid. He hadn't seen her in almost a decade. Besides, the odds stacked against him. His heart belonged to a woman completely off limits. Dylan's gaze darted to that woman's brother, his best friend, Adan. As far as he knew, Adan never suspected Dylan's secret feelings for his sister. He would do his best to make sure he never did.

Dalton kissed River after the pastor announced them as husband and wife. Dylan held back a snort. He had never even kissed his true love. Didn't know where she was. She could be married for all he knew. Adan never talked about her. Best Dylan could tell, she had no contact with her family anymore.

Seemed like what a married woman who lived out of the area might do. She probably was married. He should really stop pining over her. Give it up.

"Bro." Derin hissed from beside him.

Dylan stirred and offered his arm to his cousin Renata, River's maid of honor. Yeah, this was as close as Dylan would ever come to getting married—best man for Dalton. He figured he would watch all four of his brothers marry, eventually. Not him. Not if he couldn't find his true love. No other woman would be right for him.

As he posed for wedding party photos, he tried to soak in the experience. Hopefully, it wouldn't make his heart more lovesick.

The hours wore on. Dylan wished his brother and new sister-in-law well. Then he trudged to the bunkhouse to change out of his fancy outfit. Donning denim pants and a ratty work shirt, he ran a hand through his hair. Boots on, he left the place that would always be his home. Rooming with a bunch of bachelor men. The faces would change. He would be friends with a few. Yet friendship would do little to soothe his longing for his one true love.

Dylan flipped on the lights in the stables. The sweet scent of hay filled his lungs.

"Hey, Toffee."

He rubbed the gelding's muzzle. Horses had always been his friends. Easy to talk to. They never judged him. Never made fun of his social awkwardness. They liked his gentle voice and his astute care. Often they rewarded him with a nudge, snort, or sigh. Horses, he understood.

Women? Not even a little.

Maybe one day he would find one who put up with his tongue-tied words long enough to date him. He wouldn't hope that she would be *her*. That was just plain foolish thinking.

Dylan sighed and made his way down the row of stalls.

A verse came to mind. *With God, all things are possible.* Maybe for other people. Not for him.

Read Dylan's story in Falling for a Shy Cowboy (Vargas Ranch Book 2).

Honeymoon with a Real Cowboy

Happily ever after...
...wasn't as easy as they thought.

Seven months after their wedding, resentment and bitterness crept into their marriage. As they head to Hawaii for their postponed honeymoon, will Dalton and River mend the cracks in their marriage? Or will bizarre circumstances drive them further apart? Will a chance encounter turn them toward God and reconciliation?

Join Dalton and River Vargas on their honeymoon trip of a lifetime.

Sign up for my newsletter to get this bonus novella:
https://BookHip.com/HVKFNNP

Already a subscriber?
https://BookHip.com/TGVTNQH

From the Author

Sigh. I really love Dalton and River. They are both mature, kind people who had to overcome past relational hurt. I know rejection of any kind can be painful, so I was excited to present a story where they each learned to overcome the hurt in their own way.

The family verse and motto play an important role in each story in the series. I wanted to show how what might seem like a routine habit for the Vargas family ends up impacting people who come into their world in ways they may never know. Expect this unifying characteristic throughout the entire series.

Thank you so much for reading Dalton and River's whirlwind romance. Don't forget to pick up a free copy of their delayed honeymoon trip, with a hefty dose of reality to counteract the insta-love romance. Get these bonus scenes for free when you sign up for my newsletter. Already subscribed? Click here for your copy. If you'd rather not sign up for my newsletter, you can find *Honeymoon with a Real Cowboy* as a novella at all retailers.

Look for Dylan's story in *Falling for a Shy Cowboy (Vargas Ranch Book 2)*. He's been in love with his best friend's sister for more than a decade, so when she returns to town, he knows he must overcome his fears if he wants a chance to do that. In the process, he ends up competing with himself for her affections. How? Well, you'll have to read it to find out.

Karen Baney

About the Author

Karen Baney is passionate about writing stories full of flawed characters. She enjoys weaving together stories of second chances, redemption, and overcoming personal trials. As a transplant to Arizona, she loves researching the state's history and finding ways to seamlessly incorporate real history and real settings into her novels. In addition to writing and speaking, Karen works as a Software Development Manager for a Christian ministry.

Her faith plays an important role both in her life and in her writing. Karen and her husband, Jim, make their home in Gilbert, Arizona, with their two dogs, Bella and Daisy. Both Jim and Karen are active at Rock Point Church in Queen Creek, Arizona.

Discover faith-laced stories with characters who feel like lifelong friends.

Visit www.karenbaney.com to discover more historical romance series set in the American West. Follow Karen's writing journey and get behind-the-scenes glimpses of her research adventures on social media.

Facebook: @AuthorKarenBaney
X: @karen_baney
Instagram: @AuthorKarenBaney
BookBub: Follow Karen Baney for new release alerts

Books By Karen Baney

survival depends on grit, faith, and the courage to start over. Follow three pioneer families—the Andersons, Colters, and Larsons—as they risk everything for the promise of a new life in a land that demands both strength and hope.

A Dream Unfolding
A Heart Renewed
A Life Restored
A Hope Revealed
Hidden Prospects

Desert Manna Series:
Sometimes the most beautiful love stories bloom in the desert. Set in the growing frontier town of Prescott during the early 1870s, these tender romances follow women rebuilding their lives after heartbreak and the unexpected men who help them discover that second chances at love are worth the risk. Set in Prescott, Arizona between 1871 - 1873.

Beauty for Ashes
Joy for Mourning
Oaks of Justice

Colter Sons Series:
Power, legacy, and forbidden love collide in this sweeping family saga set in the Arizona Territory. The Colter ranch empire has weathered decades of frontier life, but now family secrets and buried betrayals threaten to destroy everything. As five brothers—and one resilient sister—navigate the treacherous waters of love, loss, and redemption, they must decide what's worth fighting for. Set in Prescott and other locations within the Arizona Territory in 1887 - 1906.

The Reluctant Cattleman
The Roaming Adventurer
The Railroad Magnate
The Resourceful Stockman
The Restless Wrangler
The Resilient Bride

Larson Sisters Series
Meet the next generation! These delightful novellas follow the three daughters of Adam and Julia Larson from the *Prescott Pioneers Series* as they navigate love, courtship, and finding their own happily ever afters in territorial Arizona in 1886 – 1894.

In Love at Christmas
In Love with the Rancher
In Love with the Horse Trainer

Desert Life Media

———

Desert Life Media: *There Is Life in The Desert*

Entertainment-first Christian fiction set in the Southwest, featuring redemption, family, and faith

Publishing clean, wholesome, and uplifting fiction since 2010

———

If you enjoyed Karen's storytelling and crave action-packed western adventure, discover R.J. Sloane's *The Rustler Hunter* at desertlifemedia.com

www.ingramcontent.com/pod-product-compliance
Lightning Source LLC
Chambersburg PA
CBHW070701280626
47159CB00022B/1761